"You have no...
and I will protect you ...
continued.

Julia's blue eyes sparked with fire. "I know I should be afraid, but I'm mad. This is our island. Our home. We can't let some cartel invade our shores. We must stop them."

Tarren stared in amazement. She was magnificent. "That's the plan. But you will have no part in it."

She tossed her hair. "We'll see about that."

He had a sinking feeling in the pit of his gut that she wasn't going to be so easy to protect. Strong-willed, stubborn and beautiful was a potent combination that was going to test all of his skills.

But he was up for the challenge.

Raz let out a series of ferocious barks.

On the shore, headed for Julia's house, were several men carrying automatic weapons.

Adrenaline flooded Tarren's veins. He launched himself at Julia, taking her to the floor. "Down!"

A barrage of gunfire peppered the house and the beachside window exploded in a rain of glass...

Terri Reed's romance and romantic suspense novels have appeared on the *Publishers Weekly* top twenty-five and NPD BookScan top one hundred lists and have been featured in *USA TODAY*, *Christian Fiction* magazine and *RT Book Reviews*. Her books have been finalists for the Romance Writers of America RITA® Award and the National Readers' Choice Award and finalists three times for the American Christian Fiction Writers Carol Award. Contact Terri at terrireed.com or PO Box 19555, Portland, OR 97224.

Books by Terri Reed

Love Inspired Suspense

Buried Mountain Secrets
Secret Mountain Hideout
Christmas Protection Detail
Secret Sabotage
Forced to Flee
Forced to Hide
Undercover Christmas Escape
Shielding the Innocent Target
Trained to Protect

Rocky Mountain K-9 Unit

Detection Detail

Pacific Northwest K-9 Unit

Explosive Trail

Mountain Country K-9 Unit

Search and Detect

Visit the Author Profile page at LoveInspired.com for more titles.

TRAINED
TO PROTECT

TERRI REED

LOVE INSPIRED SUSPENSE
INSPIRATIONAL ROMANCE

LOVE INSPIRED® SUSPENSE
INSPIRATIONAL ROMANCE

ISBN-13: 978-1-335-63857-1

Trained to Protect

Love Inspired
22 Adelaide St. West, 41st Floor
Toronto, Ontario M5H 4E3, Canada
www.LoveInspired.com

MIX
Paper | Supporting
responsible forestry
FSC® C021394

Recycling programs
for this product may
not exist in your area.

Printed in Lithuania

And every creature which is in heaven, and on the earth, and under the earth, and such as are in the sea, and all that are in them, heard I saying, Blessing, and honour, and glory, and power, be unto him that sitteth upon the throne, and unto the Lamb for ever and ever.

—*Revelation* 5:13

To Mams, the most wonderful mother-in-law
a woman could have asked for.
We love you and miss you.

ONE

"Help! Help me!"

The cry sounded from behind Julia Hamilton, and she froze, her shoes digging into the sand. Her gaze jerked away from the beach in front of her on the southern tip of South Padre Island, Texas. The wind and the rolling waves of the Gulf of Mexico could play tricks on the mind. Or...was someone really in distress?

Whirling around to stare back the way she'd just come, she lifted a hand to shield her eyes from the glare of the low springtime sun as she scanned the shoreline.

There, a hundred yards away, in the shallow space where the ocean met the sand. A dark-haired behemoth of a man wearing jeans and a baggy shirt attempted to drag a teenager dressed in workout clothes with loose blond hair into an old-school aluminum fishing boat with an out-board motor.

Earlier Julia had noticed the vessel anchored just off the shore but hadn't given it much thought.

With her adrenaline pumping and needing to do something to help the teen, Julia ran for all she was worth. Thankfully, she'd just cleared this stretch of beach for signs of turtle nests and wouldn't be treading on any turtle eggs.

"Let her go!" Julia screamed. *Please, Lord, let me get to her in time.*

She closed in on the pair, kicking up sand with her waterproof hikers. Her backpack shifted, slipping over one shoulder. She grabbed the strap and pulled it off her back but kept hold of the blue-and-yellow bag with the logo for the turtle sanctuary.

The burly man's bushy eyebrows lowered over bloodshot, dark eyes that radiated malice. He pointed a thick finger at Julia. "This is none of your business," he yelled in a thickly accented voice. "Go away."

The teenager fought against the grip the man had on her right arm. "Please! Please, help me!"

Julia splashed into the water. She pummeled the man's shoulders with her backpack. Inside the bag, the small folding shovel bounced off the guy with a tinny thud.

One beefy hand shoved Julia away, sending her onto her backside in the water. She nearly lost her grip on the backpack but managed to close her fingers tighter around the strap.

Growling with frustration and determination, Julia jumped to her feet and slung the pack over her shoulder to free her hands. She launched herself forward and wrapped her arms around the teenager's waist. Then Julia delivered a swift and accurate kick to the man's groin.

He let out a howl of rage and doubled over in pain. Julia yanked the girl from the man's grasp and sent out another kick to his bent body, toppling him into the water.

Tugging the teen onto the dry sand, Julia commanded, "Run!"

Side by side, Julia and the teen girl ran toward the parking lot.

The man's string of oaths reached them, but instead of giving chase, he jumped into the small fishing boat bobbing in the water, started the engine and sped away, disappearing around the corner of the cove.

Stopping in relief, Julia and the teenager fell to the sand several feet shy of the parking lot.

Julia wrapped her arms around the girl. She sobbed into Julia's chest. Making soothing noises and holding the teen tight with one arm, Julia grabbed her waterproof phone from the cargo pocket of her pants. She hit speed dial for her brother.

He answered on the first ring. "Jules?"

"SOS. Isla Blanca Beach. Near South Beach parking. I need you. Now!"

"Coming," came the curt reply.

Julia put the phone back in her pocket and assessed the girl who shivered in her arms. No visible injuries but that didn't mean the trauma of nearly being abducted wouldn't leave a scar. Julia had her own internal trauma scars to contend with. Brutal wounds that never really healed.

"You're safe," Julia soothed. "I won't let anyone harm you. What's your name?"

"Amber," she mumbled and continued to sob, big jerking movements that wracked her whole body.

Cold seeped into Julia's limbs but she didn't move. She'd stay like this until help arrived if doing so made Amber feel safe.

A bark drew Julia's gaze to a 120-pound black German shepherd racing toward her. Raz. The beautiful beast wore a dark vest over his lean body with the words South Padre Island Police emblazoned in silver.

Stopping next to Julia, the working K9 dog dropped to its belly with his legs tucked under him, ready to spring into action at any moment. Raz panted, his dark eyes never leaving Julia's.

Where Raz was, Tarren wasn't far behind. Julia's gaze locked on the K9 officer running toward them. Her traitorous heart gave a little thump of joy. She immediately tamped down her reaction. Now was not the time for her childhood crush to rear up to bite her. Tarren considered her only as his best friend's annoying little sister. She'd heard him say as much many times over the years.

Obviously, her brother, the police chief, had radioed his officers with her call for help. Sirens punctuated Julia's thoughts. Others would arrive on the scene soon.

Amber gave a gasp as Tarren reached them, looming like a giant oak. Out of place on a beach and unmovable.

Burrowing deeper into Julia's arms, Amber whispered, "No police."

"Too late for that," Julia said in her best no-nonsense tone. The one she used on kids who came into the turtle sanctuary for tours. "They're here to help."

Amber clung to her. "You don't understand. He'll kill us both."

Julia met Tarren's surprised gaze. The certainty in the young teen's voice sent a shiver of apprehension over Julia's flesh.

"What happened?" Tarren's tone had the same gentle one he used on skittish animals, like when they were kids.

"Attempted kidnapping," Julia said to him. "A guy in a silver fishing boat. I caught a few of the call letters. J86."

Tarren's eyebrows hitched upward over his warm, deep brown eyes. He dug into his pocket, took out a small notepad and pen, and wrote down the information. "Can you describe him?"

"Julia!" Her sole sibling, five years older, and South Padre Island's police chief, Jeremy Hamilton, pounded sand coming at them hot. He dropped to his knees next to her, his hand landing on her shoulder. "Are you okay?"

"We are." The adrenaline ebbed away, leaving Julia shivering in the early spring air. "We're cold. We need to get her somewhere warm and safe." To Tarren, she said, "I can describe the guy, but we'll do it at the station, okay?"

He nodded and put away his notepad. Standing, he held out his hand. Julia placed her wet, sandy palm against his big, warm one, ignoring how nicely they fit together. He helped Julia to her feet while Jeremy helped the teen. When Jeremy and Tarren tried to separate the teen from Julia, Amber screeched, grabbed onto Julia and clung like a barnacle.

Wrapping her arms around Amber, Julia said to the two men, "I've got her." To the teen, she said, "It's okay. Walk with me."

Though now on a leash, Raz stayed next to Julia, his body so close that he seemed to be guiding her along. Tarren had no choice but to walk on the dog's other side to keep from choking his partner, and Jeremy brought up the rear.

A news van halted a few feet from the police vehicles parked in the parking lot. A man jumped out of the passenger seat. Julia winced at the sight of the local news reporter Maxwell Street. Maxwell was joined by a cameraman who appeared to be already filming, and they were heading straight for them.

"Uh-oh," Jeremy muttered. "Max."

"How did he find out so quickly?" Tarren's tone was low and harsh.

Julia shielded Amber as best she could from the camera.

"Chief Hamilton, what happened here?" Maxwell spoke into a microphone. "The police scanner only said there was an emergency."

Well, that answered Tarren's question.

"No comment at this time," Jeremy stated in a firm tone.

Tarren met Julia's gaze. "You two ride with the chief. I'll be right behind you."

She nodded and helped Amber into the back seat of the South Padre Island police chief's cruiser, aware that her every move was being captured for the local nightly news. Apprehension twisted her insides. The would-be kidnapper had seen her just as she'd seen him.

But soon, thanks to Maxwell, he'd know exactly who she was and where to find her. Julia pushed that thought away as she settled in the police cruiser.

The ride to the police station took all of ten minutes with the way Jeremy drove. Sirens blared, forcing the late afternoon traffic to split so they could pass through the town of South Padre unimpeded. The familiar shops and restaurants of the resort town on either side of Padre Boulevard passed by in a blur. Julia kept her focus on the teen who shivered in her arms beneath the space blanket Jeremy had wrapped them in.

He pulled around to the back of the police station and hustled them inside, straight to his office.

"We're going to need your statements." Jeremy's gaze pinned Julia to the leather couch where she and the teenager sat. Compassion filled his eyes. "Let me get you ladies something warm to drink. I'll be right back."

Julia sank back into the cushions and nodded.

Jeremy ducked out the door, closing it softly behind him.

Amber pulled away from Julia. "We shouldn't be here. What if that man comes after me again?"

Julia thought better than to argue. The girl was in crisis mode. Keeping her tone soft and modulated, Julia said, "You are safe here. My brother, the police chief, and his best friend, Tarren, the K9 officer, will not let anything happen to either of us. All of the police officers here will protect us."

The certainty in her tone must have persuaded the girl. She sat back on the couch, grabbing a small throw pillow and hugging it to her chest. "I want my parents."

"Are they here in town?"

"Yes. We're renting a home in Gravity Park," the girl said.

The door opened and Tarren and Raz walked in. The pair made for a striking picture. Both were strong and athletic with well-defined muscles. Tarren was so handsome with his dark close-cropped hair and warm brown eyes. Raz's dark eyes nearly matched his black fur, which matched the color of his K9 vest. Raz left his handler's side and came to Julia, putting his snout on her knee.

Tarren raised an eyebrow but didn't call his dog off.

Julia tore her gaze away from Tarren and met Raz's intent doggy gaze. Rubbing him behind the ears, she said, "Amber needs to call her parents."

"That can be arranged." Tarren handed Amber his notebook and pen. "I'll need you to write down their contact info."

Amber jotted down the details and handed the notepad and pen back.

Armed with the notepad, Tarren walked to the door and waved over a uniformed patrol officer. "Daniel, go to this address and bring these people to the station. Tell them their daughter is okay, but she needs them here."

The officer nodded and hurried away.

Tarren moved to a chair facing the couch. "Amber, can you explain to me what happened?"

A shudder visibly went through Amber.

Julia scooted closer and put an arm around her shoulders. "You can trust him."

Tarren made a small noise in his throat, drawing her attention. The way he stared at her caused a heated flush to chase away the last of the chill from the ocean water.

"I'm training for a decathlon at home in Tennessee," Amber said. "I was out for my morning run."

Focusing on the Amber, he asked, "Do you go the same way every time?"

"Yes." She blinked back tears. "My father helped me map out a five-mile route that didn't take me far from our vacation home. We thought it would be safe."

The door to the office opened and Jeremy walked in with two steaming mugs of hot chocolate loaded with mini marshmallows. Just the way Julia loved it. She smiled her thanks, and she took the mug. Amber held hers in her hand but didn't drink from the chocolaty goodness.

Jeremy hitched a hip on the side of his desk. "You can continue. Don't mind me."

Tarren gave him a nod, then turned his gaze back to Amber. "Have you ever seen the man before?"

Amber shook her head. "Not that I recall. But I honestly don't pay much attention to my surroundings when I'm in the zone."

Julia figured that would change now that Amber had experienced this trauma.

Tarren's gaze turned to Julia. "Have *you* ever seen him?"

She thought about that. Having grown up on South Padre Island, she was aware of most of the locals. Though the island and the town had grown into a tourist destination, it was also a small town in many ways. Those who called South Padre Island home watched out for each other. Until now, Julia had always thought herself safe here. "He wasn't from the island. But with all the tourists we get—" She shrugged. "I've never seen him in the sanctuary."

Her workplace attracted tourists and locals alike. Safe Haven Turtle Sanctuary, a rescue and rehabilitation center for the many varieties of sea turtles that inhabited the ocean, also provided educational workshops and tours of the facility, as well as protected the turtle nests and managed the public hatchings every year on the island's various beaches. Julia had fallen in love with the work as a kid. She'd known exactly what her path would be. In college, she majored in marine biology and conservationism so that she could return to the island to work for the sanctuary.

"Would you be willing to sit with a forensic artist?" Jeremy asked.

Julia raised her eyebrows in surprise. "I didn't know we had one on the island."

"A new hire," Jeremy explained. "Officer Stacy Ridgefield comes to us from Boston. She's an artist. I'll have her come in."

Jeremy moved around the back of the desk and hit the button on the phone. The police station's receptionist, Blanche Goodfried, answered, "Yes, Chief?"

"Can you send Officer Ridgefield to my office?" Jeremy asked. "And tell her to bring her artist tools."

"Right away."

Jeremy clicked off.

"So, you went jogging today down by the jetty," Tarren prompted. "When did the man grab you?"

"I didn't see him at first," Amber said, her voice shaking. "But he jumped out from behind a berm as I was heading back toward the parking lot. He grabbed me and tried to—" She buried her head in the pillow.

"She screamed and I heard it," Julia said, rubbing circles on the teen's back. "I had just cleared that stretch of beach and had seen the boat but not the man. I ran to help."

"Did the man say anything?" Jeremy asked.

"He said it was none of my business and to go away," Julia told them. "When I got her away from him, he let out a string of curse words in English and Spanish. The Spanish I didn't understand."

"He said he'd kill us in Spanish," Amber interjected, her tone nearing hysteria.

A lump of dread formed in Julia's throat. She swallowed before saying, "He may have said that. Honestly, I wasn't paying attention to him. I was more concerned about escaping."

"And how did you get away from him?" Jeremy asked.

Julia made a face.

Amber piped up, "She kicked him in the...you know where."

Jeremy and Tarren grinned at each other.

"A tactic that has served you well," Jeremy observed.

Julia barely refrained from rolling her eyes at her brother. He was the one who taught her how to defend herself if she was ever attacked. His go-to advice had always been to first go for the groin, then the eyes, then the throat. She loved him for that. While her parents had been as attentive and caring as possible, they had been busy with their careers, their mother an ob-gyn and their father a cardiologist. Once Jeremy had been old enough, he'd been her main babysitter growing up. She'd trailed after him to his baseball practices, his games and whatever else he and Tarren were involved in. It made for some fun and exciting adventures but also, she knew her brother had resented having to care for her so much, which had caused them to fight often as children.

There was a knock at the office door.

Jeremy called, "Come in."

The door opened to reveal a female uniformed patrol officer. Her midnight-black hair was slicked back into a tight bun. She wore a liberal layer of makeup, making Julia wonder if she was covering acne scars. Her dark eyes, behind a pair of thick glasses, skimmed over Julia and Amber before focusing on Jeremy. She had a satchel slung over her shoulder. "Chief?"

Jeremy rose from his desk and came around to gesture at Julia and Amber. "Stacy, we need you to sit with my sister and this young lady to do a sketch composite of their attacker."

Stacy's dark eyes flared, and she nodded. "I can do that." She moved past Jeremy and Tarren with a nod and pulled up a side chair so that she was sitting next to the couch. She set the satchel on the floor and brought out a sketch pad and charcoal pencils. "Ladies, shall we begin?"

Remembering a true-crime show she'd watched last year, Julia said, "I thought composites were done on a computer."

"Sometimes," Stacy replied with a patient smile. "I prefer this way. At least to start with. If we need to, we'll jump to the composite software on my laptop." She indicated the satchel.

"We're not needed here," Jeremy said to Tarren and stepped out of the office.

Julia glanced up at Tarren, her breath catching at the look in his eyes. She didn't know how to decipher what she observed there. Concern, protectiveness, annoyance?

Memories of all the times she'd chased after Jeremy and Tarren on their escapades crowded her brain. Back then, Tarren had displayed a similar expression, only today there was something else lurking in his gaze that she didn't understand.

He gave her a sharp nod and then clicked into his cheek, summoning Raz. But the dog didn't move. He stared at his handler and then back at Julia.

Tarren cocked his head.

Julia was quick to say, "Can he stay? He makes me feel safe."

Tarren's mouth quirked, the sides dimpling. "Of course. I'll collect him in a bit."

Shaking his head, Tarren walked out of the office, closing the door behind him. Julia bit the inside of her lip. It was all she could do not to ask him to stay as well. He'd always made her feel safe and cared for. More so than her own brother at times.

She bent forward to place a kiss on Raz's head between his eyes. "You're a good boy."

* * *

Tarren joined Jeremy in the station's break room. Tables and chairs were set up around the space. A coffee maker gurgled on the counter. A refrigerator hummed in the corner. A box of doughnuts beckoned.

Jeremy raised an eyebrow. "Raz?"

"With your sister." Tarren grabbed a glazed old-fashioned doughnut and munched on it.

His dog was taken with Julia. So was he if he were being honest. He was proud of her for coming to Amber's rescue and for thinking so quickly on her feet. He was thankful neither Julia nor Amber had been harmed. And hearing Julia state she thought him trustworthy had filled Tarren with an odd sort of warmth that settled near his heart.

Jeremy chuckled. "She's always had a soft spot for animals."

After swallowing his bite, Tarren said, "Hence why she became an animal biologist."

"Marine biologist, but still…" Pouring himself a cup of coffee, Jeremy asked, "What do you make of this attempted kidnapping?"

Tarren had a sinking sensation in his gut. "I don't like it. It makes me wonder if—"

"—the two missing girls are related," Jeremy finished.

Tarren nodded. It had always been that way between them. They could finish each other's thoughts without trying. He supposed they were closer than brothers since neither of them had a brother.

They only had Julia.

Jeremy's little sister had followed them around like a lost puppy, always getting in the way and messing up their fun. But she'd grown into a beautiful, competent and respected woman.

The first time Tarren had seen her when she'd returned to the island after college, he'd nearly dropped the coffee he just purchased at the local diner. She'd walked in like she owned the place. Gone were the long light red braids framing her oval face and the braces she'd been sporting when Tarren and Jeremy had graduated from high school.

Tarren hadn't been at Julia's high school graduation, or her college graduation, even though he'd been invited. Those had been the dark years with his mom. Who was he kidding? They were all dark years. But those four years between Julia's graduation dates had been the worst. Then his mother passed, releasing him from the anguish of watching her drink herself to death.

Seeing Julia today, wet and scared, had gutted him. He hated to think what would've happened if that man had had accomplices. Both Amber and Julia might have been taken. A simmering anger low in his gut had his stomach roiling and made the doughnut he'd just eaten seem like a brick in his abdomen.

He gave his head a shake, turning his thoughts back to the question lingering in the air. *Is someone targeting young women on South Padre Island?*

TWO

"I've got a bad feeling," Jeremy said, which only amplified the churning in Tarren's insides. "We need to do a deep dive into the other two disappearances."

"Our investigation into both young women's disappearances hit walls. We should get the FBI involved in the runaway case," Tarren said. "If she was kidnapped instead of running away as her parents claim, the Feds could search for her on the mainland."

Jeremy nodded. "Good idea. I'll also reach out to the Coast Guard to look for the boat and ask them to do another sweep around the island, searching for any signs of the girl who supposedly drowned near the jetty. If she really did disappear in the water, we may never find her."

"We can only do our best and pray that God will lead us to the answers," Tarren said with conviction deep in his chest.

"Indeed."

They fell silent for a moment. No way was

Tarren going to let Julia become the kidnapper's target.

"Will you—" Jeremy began.

"I'm not letting her out of my sight," Tarren finished the thought.

Jeremy grinned. "You know she'll balk."

Tarren grinned back. "Too bad. Her safety will be our priority."

Jeremy moved toward the door and patted Tarren on the back as he passed. "I don't envy you, but I do thank you. Even if she won't."

"You and your family were there for me more times than I can count," Tarren replied, following Jeremy out of the break room. "It's the least I can do."

Now Tarren just had to figure out a way to make this all okay with Julia.

"Yes, that's him." Julia stared at the composite drawing that Officer Stacy Ridgefield had drawn from the description given by Julia and Amber. The sketch was so lifelike, depicting the broad flat face, and a nose that had probably been broken more than once. The dark low hairline and thick eyebrows over hooded dark eyes.

A shudder, born of fear and revulsion, worked through Julia. Raz nuzzled her as if offering comfort. The heat of his body pressed against her leg soothed and redirected her focus to Amber, who also confirmed the image Stacy was holding up.

Amber nodded, her eyes welling with tears. "I'll never forget his mean face."

Julia put an arm around the girl's shoulders. "The police will catch him." She turned her gaze to Stacy. "What happens now?"

"I'll give the composite to the chief," Stacy said. "He'll know what to do with it."

"Which is?" Julia pressed.

The door to Jeremy's office opened. Tarren and Jeremy filed through it.

Stacy rose from the chair and handed Jeremy the drawing. "The ladies would like to know what you'll do with the drawing."

"We'll send this composite out to all law enforcement agencies in the country," Jeremy said. "And run his image through every database we have access to. We need to identify him first, then we'll go after him."

"What do we do while waiting for you to identify and go after this guy?" Julia asked, her gaze skipping to Tarren where he stood with his arms crossed over his chest. He appeared very confident and relaxed. The two things she didn't feel at the moment. Resentment bubbled in her blood. She squashed the emotion. It wasn't his fault she was upset. The blame lay at the feet of the man who'd tried to abduct Amber.

"Until then," Jeremy said with a shrug, "you live your life. Both of you."

"I'm not running by myself, ever again," Amber said.

Julia squeezed her shoulders. She hated that Amber was now afraid to do something she loved.

Blanche, Jeremy's administrative assistant, stepped into the doorway. Her graying hair curled around her head like a halo. "Mr. and Mrs. Lynn are here."

Amber jumped up. "Can I see my parents now?"

"Blanche, have them come in, please," Jeremy said.

A well-dressed, handsome couple in their late forties stepped into the office. Their gazes locked directly on their daughter. The relief on Mr. Lynn's face was palpable. He was a big man, with broad linebacker shoulders, and he moved with athletic grace. Tears welled in Mrs. Lynn's green eyes. The resemblance between mother and daughter was strong. Both were tall, lithe and pretty with blond hair and high cheekbones.

Amber let out a squeal and ran into their waiting arms.

The three-way hug made Julia long for her own parents. She decided she would go see them soon, instead of waiting for their Sunday night dinner.

In her quest to be an independent adult she hadn't explained the breakup with her boyfriend of five years, Bryce Basel, on graduation night. She'd kept that humiliation to herself. She was still licking her wounds and needed time to heal.

Never again would she be dumb enough to trust a man so easily. If, and that was a big *if*, she ever went down the romance road again, she'd be the one in control and not believe the promises and lies that seemed to come so easily to men like Bryce.

Jeremy waited a beat, letting the family rejoice in being together. Julia appreciated her brother's patience. Why couldn't she find someone steady and trustworthy like her brother? Her gaze strayed to Tarren. She quickly jerked her focus back to Amber and her parents. Her fingers smoothed through Raz's fur.

Finally, Jeremy stepped forward, interrupting the reunion. He held out his hand to the father. "Mr. Lynn, I'm Chief Hamilton. Your daughter, as you can see, is safe and unharmed."

"That's what the officer told us," Mrs. Lynn said. "But I'm glad to see it's true."

"What happens now, Chief Hamilton?" Mr. Lynn kept an arm around his daughter and moved to sandwich her between him and his wife.

"We will inform you of any development. Until this man is caught, I will make sure we patrol the area of your vacation home while you are on the island," Jeremy promised.

"Oh, that won't be necessary," Mrs. Lynn said, her voice quaking with what could only be called anger. "We are leaving this island as soon as we get back to the vacation rental. We are booked on the next flight out of Corpus Christi."

Julia refrained from saying she thought that was wise. The man who'd targeted Amber might come after her again, if for no other reason than she'd seen his face. But Julia kept the thought to herself, just as she was sure her brother and Tarren were both doing.

"If you could leave your contact information with the front desk," Tarren said, "we'll give you a police escort to the mainland."

"Of course." Mr. Lynn's gaze swept from Jeremy to Tarren to Julia and stayed. "The officer told us you helped our daughter."

Julia stood. "I did what anyone would do."

Mrs. Lynn hurried forward and engulfed Julia in a hug. "You're a hero."

A protest rose on Julia's tongue, but she bit the words back.

Once Mrs. Lynn disengaged, Mr. Lynn stepped forward, extending his hand.

Feeling self-conscious from the attention, Julia shook the man's hand.

"Young lady, if you need anything, you just let us know," Mr. Lynn said.

"I'm good, honestly," Julia said, extracting her hand from the older gentleman's. "I'm just glad Amber is safe with you now."

"That she is," Mr. Lynn said. "Thank you, all of you."

He ushered his family out of Jeremy's office. Through the glass plate window separating Jeremy's office from the front desk, Julia watched the family. They stopped to give Blanche their contact information. Amber met Julia's gaze and offered her a small smile and wave. Julia waved back, with a nod and a smile. Then the Lynns left the police station.

"I need a ride back to my car," Julia said into the quiet of the office. Her gaze met her brother's.

Jeremy nodded his chin toward Tarren. "We figured as much."

"I've got you," Tarren said. He snapped his fingers, drawing Raz away from her side. "Let me clock out for the night and we'll take you over."

Julia frowned. "You don't have to do this on your off-duty time. I'm sure my brother can manage to get me back to Isla Blanca Park."

"No can do," Jeremy said with a shrug.

"What happened?" Her gaze bounced between the two men. "Tarren, did you pick the short straw of protection duty?"

The two men grinned at each other. Some private joke passed between them.

"Something like that," Tarren said. "We'll bring the vehicle around front."

He and Raz walked out of the office. She watched them move fluidly through the lobby and disappear down the hall toward the locker rooms. She whirled on her brother. "Seriously, you can't drive me over?"

He pinned her with an intense gaze, making her want to squirm. She held her ground, not about to let him intimidate her. He may be older and bigger, but she'd inherited their paternal grandmother's steel spine. Her father's mother had raised four kids alone after her husband's unexpected death due to a heart condition, which had prompted their father to become a heart doctor.

"I have to run this guy's mug," he said, waving the charcoal-drawn image at her. "Let Tarren get you to your rig and back to your place. I'll stop by when I'm done."

"I'm going to the sanctuary," she told him. "I need to explain my absence to my boss."

"I'm sure a phone call will suffice," he charged back.

"I'll call but I need to go to the sanctuary," she insisted, making her voice as hard as she could. "I have responsibilities there. And my purse is in my locker along with my house keys and wallet."

He broke eye contact, walked around his desk and sat down. "That's between you and Tarren. I'll check in with you later."

His dismissal was as acute as if he'd actually said the words. She made a face at his bent head over his computer keyboard. She stomped out of the room. Her brother's low, mocking chuckle followed. Her steps faltered and she threw a glare over her shoulder. He ignored her. Brothers.

True to his word, Tarren was waiting outside, standing next to the passenger side of his vehicle. He opened the door for her. She moved to climb in, and his hand gripped her elbow, his touch warm through the fabric of her damp shirt. She pressed her lips together to keep from saying she didn't need his help. He was being a gentleman. She couldn't fault him for his manners. She wasn't even sure why she was upset. Next to Jeremy, Tarren was the only other person she would trust her safety to on the island. Or anywhere for that matter.

She sat in silence as they drove back to Isla Blanca Park's parking lot. He slowed the vehicle a few feet away from the Safe Haven Turtle Sanctuary's truck.

Julia jumped out of the police vehicle as Tarren pulled the lever that popped open the side compartment door, letting Raz hop out. "I need to clear the truck before you drive it."

"Don't you think you're being paranoid?"

"Better safe than—"

"Sorry," she finished his thought. "I get it." Though she didn't think he'd find anything worrisome.

Tarren climbed out of the SUV, hooked up his partner and they cautiously approached the blue-and-white truck with the colorful Safe Haven logo on the side panels. Julia stayed back a few feet and watched, fascinated by the two working as one. She couldn't help but admire the pair as Tarren motioned for Raz to sniff all the way around the vehicle.

She'd always respected Tarren's sense of duty. There had been times when Jeremy had wanted to ditch her, but Tarren had spoken up, saying it was their job to watch out for her.

Taking out her cell phone, she called her boss, Pattie, and filled her in on what was happening.

Pattie was understandably concerned. "Are you safe?"

"Yes. I'll be over soon to take care of the girls," Julia promised and hung up, her gaze riveted on Raz, who sat near the driver's side door and let out a loud bark.

Then Tarren dropped to his hands and knees to check under the vehicle. He scrambled away from the truck, tugging Raz with him, and hustled back to where she sat waiting with her heart in her throat.

Raz had alerted on something. And whatever it was, it wasn't good judging by the ashen expression on Tarren's face.

Tarren thumbed his radio attached to his uniform, letting dispatch know they needed to send the police department's crime scene investigation team and the lone bomb tech to Isla Blanca

Park's parking lot. He'd been right to approach Julia's work vehicle with caution.

Someone had attached an explosive device to the undercarriage on the driver's side.

And he would hazard a guess it was rigged to explode when the engine turned over. Part of his and Raz's training had included differentiating various types of explosives and devices.

"What is it?"

"Car bomb." Obviously, the man who'd attempted to abduct Amber was trying to silence Julia. Once he realized that she and Amber were able to give a composite sketch of their attacker's face, the man would either disappear or come after Julia and Amber with a vengeance. His chest constricted with dread.

She stared at him, horror in her blue eyes. "That kind of thing doesn't happen here."

He hated to be the one to tell her violence could happen anywhere. Even their small town island.

She clutched the sleeve of his uniform and pointed to the berm several yards away. "It's him."

Silhouetted with the sun at his back, a large man, whose features were in shadow, stood watching them. In his hand he held what appeared to be a detonator. Alarm slammed into Tarren. He grabbed Julia around the waist, hauling her off her feet.

Carrying Julia, he ran toward the safety of his

vehicle just as the Safe Haven truck exploded. The force sent him to his knees with Julia in his arms. He curled around her, taking the blast of heat buffeting his back.

"Raz!" Tarren's gaze whipped around, searching for his partner.

Raz had shimmied beneath the K9 unit vehicle, his dark eyes piercing in the glow of the fire engulfing the sanctuary truck.

Tarren thumbed the radio at his shoulder. "10-80," he said, giving the code for an explosion. "Officer needs assistance."

He turned to see if the bomber was nearby, but the man had disappeared over the other side of the berm.

Tarren released Julia and helped her to her feet. They brushed off the sand. "You're not going to your house alone."

She made a noise in her throat, a half scoff, half sob. "You think? Obviously, he's trying to prevent me from identifying him. Too late."

Tarren wasn't surprised her quick mind had come up with the same answer he had. She was a marvel, this one. She had always been way too smart for her own good. Smarter than all of them. He'd never doubted she would make a good life for herself doing something in the sciences.

Every year, for as long as he could remember, she'd won the science fair contest. Even the year when she went to a NASA convention in Corpus Christi. What did surprise him was that she wasn't in the NASA program. But then again, her love of animals apparently had overridden any other dreams.

He opened the passenger door of his SUV. "Get in. We'll wait inside until the crime scene unit and bomb tech arrive."

She didn't hesitate but scrambled back into the passenger seat.

"I didn't realize Raz was a bomb-sniffing dog," she said.

"He's multi-trained on every discipline, being our one and only canine dog for the whole police department," he said, trying not to let his frustration color his words.

"Why only one dog? Shouldn't there be more?"

He heaved a sigh as he closed the passenger side door, making sure she was securely inside. He glanced around, searching for a threat, before he walked to the driver's side and motioned for Raz to jump into his compartment. Tarren took his time shutting the door and opening the driver's door. How did he answer her question without throwing shade at anyone?

"We're a small department," he finally said. "The fundraiser we did to buy Raz barely covered his fee. And the bi-quarterly training is a stretch on the department's budget."

"Who's in charge of funding?" she asked.

He made a face.

"What?"

"The city council," he said.

"Wait. My dad's on the council."

He lifted a shoulder but didn't comment. The information was easily obtained with a search on the internet.

She let out a harrumph and crossed her arms over her chest.

Still, he didn't want her thinking badly of her father. "I'm sure your dad went to bat for us to get Raz and permission to do the fundraiser," Tarren told her. Though he didn't really have proof. He and Jeremy had both decided to keep a cone of silence between the department and the city council, including Mr. Hamilton. Easier to keep the peace that way.

The CSI team and the bomb tech arrived within minutes. Jeremy, as well.

Tarren caught Julia's gaze. "Stay put." The last thing he needed was her out in the open. This guy who was after her was bold and Tarren didn't want to take any chances.

She saluted him. The gesture was so reminiscent of when she was a kid that he busted out with a laugh. Shaking his head, he reminded himself she wasn't a kid. She'd turned into a woman with curves and a mind of her own. A woman to be reckoned with. Deciding to ensure she stayed in the vehicle, he opened the dog door between the front compartment and Raz's compartment. The dog climbed halfway through and started licking Julia's face.

"I know what you're doing," she said between laughing and trying to fend off Raz.

"I've no idea what you're talking about," he quipped and jumped out to talk to her brother.

After he explained what Raz had discovered, the crime scene investigation team, along with the bomb tech, went to work.

"I'll manage this. You get my sister out of here," Jeremy said. "Take her to my parents. I'll come by after work."

"You're the chief." Tarren returned to his SUV and sent up a silent prayer of protection over Jeremy and the team. He started the engine and headed them out of the parking lot back toward town.

"Will they be safe?"

"Yes," he replied with confidence. "I doubt the bomber will return, but Jeremy will have officers comb the beach for any traces of him."

"I need to go to the sanctuary," she said.

"Not happening."

"Yes, happening," she insisted. "I need to let my boss know what is going on so that she can take precautions. Plus, I have things at the sanctuary I need to do. And my wallet and house keys are in my locker."

"I'm taking you to your parents," Tarren told her. "You can call your boss from there. Please don't make this any more difficult than it has to be."

She buried her face in Raz's fur. "You haven't changed a bit. Just as bossy as ever."

"Better bossy than letting something happen to my best friend's little sister." He needed the reminder she was off-limits because all he really wanted to do was take her in his arms and tell her he would keep her safe no matter what.

THREE

Hiding her face in Raz's dark fur, Julia made another expression of displeasure. Hearing Tarren restate exactly how he considered her even after all these years stung. It was just as well. She had no intention of lowering her guard and letting someone in who could break her heart again.

Tarren could do that.

She'd had a crush on him as a kid and now seeing him as an adult—well—she forced her mind away from thoughts of how handsome and mature he was now at thirty-five. The past was done and her attraction to him had to be over as well.

His bossiness may have worked on her when she was a kid, but she was an adult with her own mind and her own agency. Never again would she let anyone dictate her life. She'd let Bryce have too much say in how she spent her time while they were together.

She sat up straight, releasing Raz. "I will go to my parents' after we visit the sanctuary. I need to talk to my boss and grab my house keys and wallet. Then we will stop by my house so I can pack a bag. I don't have any clothes that fit anymore at my parents."

Tarren glanced at her with a frown over Raz's head.

If he said anything about the twenty pounds she'd lost since the last time she lived at home, she was going to smack him in the shoulder just like she had when she was a kid. Her fingers curled in her lap.

"Julia, this is not a—"

She held up a hand, stopping his words. "Do you believe that you and Raz can protect me?"

His frown deepened. "Of course I do."

She gestured with her hands in the air. Raz sniffed at her fingers. "Well, then. It shouldn't be a problem to stop at the sanctuary. We won't stay long. Nor will stopping at my house be an issue as long as you're confident you can protect me."

His nostrils flared, a sure sign he was angry.

Oh, she'd done it now. She lifted her chin and waited. Raz must have sensed his handler's change in mood because he backed up and disappeared inside his compartment.

Back in the day, Jeremy and Tarren had been good at harassing her into submission. Which was probably why she'd fallen so easily for Bryce's manipulations. But she'd gone through a year of therapy after breaking up with him, before returning to the island. She was stronger and surer of herself now. Or at least that's what she hoped. Testing her newfound self-esteem on Tarren seemed safe.

Especially since there could never be anything between them romantically. He was just her older brother's best friend. Nothing more. And just because she'd always had a thing for him didn't mean she had one now.

"Look," Tarren said. "I promised Jeremy I would take you straight to your parents'."

"And Jeremy told me I had to negotiate with you about going to the sanctuary," she replied. Of course, that had been before they found the bomb attached to her work truck. But Tarren didn't need to know that.

Tarren cocked his head. "And just when did he say this?"

Busted. "Does it matter? You're going to protect me, right?"

It was his turn to make a face.

For a moment, she thought he'd ignore her challenge but then he turned off Padre Boulevard onto the side street that would lead them to the Safe Haven Turtle Sanctuary.

She pressed her lips together to keep her satisfaction from spreading into a grin. It was a small victory, but she would take it anyway. Besides, she had every confidence she would be safe with him and Raz by her side.

He pulled into the parking lot of the sanctuary, choosing a space right next to the door, and turned off the engine. The building was painted sea-foam green with a beautiful, spray-painted mural of a Kemp's ridley turtle and other sea life. The renowned artist had donated his talent, and the stunning image always brought a smile to Julia's face.

"You will stay by my side the whole time."

Tarren's words jerked her gaze from the art covering the front of the sanctuary. The serious expression on his face made her stomach quiver. The intensity of his brown eyes held her captive. He really was a handsome man. She noted the tiny scar above his right eyebrow and wondered how he'd acquired it.

"You will let me enter the door first and exit the door first," he continued.

Swallowing a rising tide of anxiety, she held up her hands, palms out. "Of course. You're the boss." At least for now. "I'm not reckless. I fully intend to let you do your job."

"Okay, then," he said. "Stay put. I will come around and walk you to the door."

She nodded and sent up a plea to God that nothing would happen while they were at the sanctuary. She really didn't want any of her co-workers or her boss to be hurt because of what she'd gotten herself mixed up in.

Tarren climbed out and opened the back compartment for Raz. Once he had the dog on a leash, they walked around to the passenger side door. He opened it and held out his hand.

She slipped her much smaller hand into his, their palms meeting in a rush of sensation that traveled up her arm. On reflex, her fingers tightened around his and she allowed him to help her down from the SUV. Then he tucked her into his side in a protective gesture that was both endearing and a bit overwhelming. His head swiveled back and forth, his gaze, no doubt, searching for a threat as he hustled her to the sanctuary entrance.

True to his word, Tarren entered first but moved aside so she and Raz could join him. Once inside, he paused, keeping her close. When he seemed satisfied that no danger lurked inside the warehouse-sized facility, he released his hold on her.

She missed his hand on her waist. Shaking off the ridiculous notion, she moved forward toward the offices.

Her boss rushed out of her office.

Pattie Whittier was a petite woman in her early seventies. She had short, curly gray hair that framed a round face sporting equally round bifocals. Over her knit pants and long-sleeved shirt, she wore a dark blue rubber apron they all wore when tending to the turtles.

Pattie wrapped her arms around Julia. "I've been so worried since you called. I sent everyone else home. It's been on the news. That must've been so scary. But it was a good thing you were out there today. Or that poor girl might've—" Pattie gave a visible shudder.

Extracting herself from the hug and grasping Pattie's hands, Julia said, "Yes, it was horrifying. But also, a good thing. I am safe and the girl is safe, too."

Peering at her intensely from behind her bifocals, Pattie said, "Are you, though? The news just reported your Safe Haven vehicle exploded."

Julia groaned. Of course, Maxwell, the local news reporter, would've been on top of his scanner and eager to tell the world there'd been a bomb, but she was still alive. Anxiety ate away at her gut. No time to think of the bomb or the attacker now. She had things to do so she and Tarren could leave. "I'm sure insurance will cover the cost of the truck."

Pattie gasped. "So, it's true. I thought for sure Maxwell was making that part up. I'm just glad you're okay."

Smothering a sigh, Julia said, "He's just doing his job. I'm going to grab my purse. You should leave, too."

"I was about to feed the girls," Pattie said.

"I'll take care of them," Julia said. "Tarren's here. You go on."

Taking off the apron and handing it over, Pattie said, "Are you sure?"

"Yes," Julia insisted as she took hold of the apron.

"Only for the rest of the day?" Pattie asked, her gaze going to Tarren. "Surely tomorrow we can open."

Julia turned to Tarren as well. "I have a school tour tomorrow."

"Definitely cancel the tour," Tarren said. "Let me talk to the chief about getting you some security here before you open back up to the public."

Pattie frowned. "I'll clear the calendar for the rest of the week."

Julia hated how this was impacting the sanctuary. "But you'll call me if you need me?"

Pattie smiled. "Of course I will."

"You promise? If a turtle is in distress, I want to know."

Holding up her hands in acquiescence, Pattie said, "I promise I will call you if there are any turtles in distress."

Hugging the older woman again, Julia said, "I'm so sorry about all of this."

"Not your fault, dear." Pattie smiled. "I'll lock up behind me."

Pattie returned to her office, grabbed her purse and left the sanctuary, locking the front door behind her.

Aware of Tarren's gaze, Julia donned the water-resistant apron. When she glanced up, she saw thunderclouds in his brown eyes.

Realizing she was pushing his sense of duty to the limit, she led the way to the large tank in the middle of what they called the exhibit room. There were benches all the way around the middle tank where the three turtles lived.

"This won't take long, I promise," she said.

Tarren grunted out a response.

She took that as acceptance and went about the task of feeding the turtles while Tarren and Raz watched. Needing to fill the silence, she explained the girls' history and the food they were eating. "When turtles come to us for rehabilitation, the goal is to get them back out in the wild. But it doesn't always work. Sophie was missing her tail and her back right flipper when she was brought in. Both had been caught in a fisherman's net and had had to be amputated. However, she now has a prosthetic flipper that allows her to swim. But releasing her would be risky so she lives here."

"Prosthetic?" Tarren moved in for a closer look. Raz appeared uninterested in the turtle tank. He lay down and watched them.

"Sophie is a green sea turtle, and she adores green peppers and squid," Julia said as she doled out chunks of both from a bucket marked with the turtle's name.

"What about this one?" Tarren pointed to a smaller turtle.

"That is Kate," Julia said and picked up the

bucket with Kate's name. "She likes shrimp and crab. Very upper crust, you know." She put chunks of the shellfish into the tank and Kate attacked the food with gusto.

Tarren's chuckle rumbled in his chest and Julia paused. She liked the way his eyes crinkled at the corners when he laughed.

Turning back to watch Kate, Julia said, "She was born with only half of the front left flipper. We released her into the ocean, but she washed back up on shore a few hours later. There was no way she'd survive in the wild, so she came here. The kids love her. She travels well when taken to public events and schools."

The third turtle swam near waiting for her food.

"This is Bridget," Julia said as she grabbed the next bucket filled with more green peppers and crab. "Her shell had been cracked when she'd been cold-stunned and had smacked against the rocky jetty at the southern tip of the island."

"Cold-stunned?"

"When the water temperatures drop to fifty degrees or less, the turtles' heart rate and circulation decrease, causing lethargy. Which can lead to shock, pneumonia, frostbite and, potentially death, as they aren't able to migrate to warmer waters."

"Can they be warmed up?"

"Sure. Many are. But if there's damage... We keep them here where they can thrive."

"This is quite an operation you have here," Tarren said. "I'm impressed."

"Don't you remember coming here as a kid?"

Tarren shrugged. But he didn't answer.

Her curiosity piqued, Julia decided if she and Tarren were going to be spending time together while her brother hunted down the guy who'd tried to kidnap Amber, Julia wanted to get to know the man to whom she was entrusting her life.

Tarren was thankful Julia let him dodge her question about having visited the turtle sanctuary when they were kids. He remembered when his fifth-grade class went on the sanctuary field trip. His mother had been passed out on the couch with vomit all over her, an empty bottle of whiskey and an empty bottle of vodka on the table next to her. He'd stayed home making her coffee and food instead of going on the field trip. She'd written him a note saying he was the one who had been sick.

Only Jeremy knew the truth. And Tarren had sworn Jeremy to secrecy.

Even at a young age, Tarren understood if the adults in their lives found out his mother was drunk and incapable of taking care of herself, let alone him, he would've been removed from the home. He'd been afraid his mother might've killed herself. The drinking eventually did the job but not until much later.

Shaking off thoughts of his past, he was fascinated with all that Julia had told him about the sanctuary and the resident turtles. He and Raz followed her into the women's locker room, where she grabbed her purse and a few other items that she put in a shopping bag.

He put his hand on Julia's lower back and nudged her toward the exit. After she unlocked the door, he went out first, paused, scanning the area, but detected no immediate threat. Julia came out and locked the door behind them. Once they were all secure in the SUV, he drove to the small beach cottage where Julia lived.

"So, you know where I live and you've never visited," she said, the words sounding like an accusation laced with hurt.

"I haven't been invited," he countered.

"Fair enough," she said. "Well, you're invited now."

He put a staying hand on her arm. "The same rules apply here."

"Yep, got it." Her words were tempered with a grin that did funny things to his insides.

He hopped out, released Raz and then went around to open the passenger door for Julia. She held out her hand before he had a chance to hold out his. Taking her hand in his, he was once again struck by her strong grip as he helped her from the SUV. Not that she needed the help. The woman was agile and had always been athletic.

Tucking her close to his side again, breathing in the scent of the salt water clinging to her clothes and hair, he said, "If you want to freshen up while we're here, I think that will be fine."

She tilted her face up and pursed her lips before saying, "Fine? As in frantic, indignant, nauseous and entertaining?"

He snorted out a laugh. "I'm not sure those go together."

They paused on the doorstep to allow her to fit her key in the lock. Keeping her behind him, he entered, stopping to allow his senses to assess any threats or danger. The house was quiet, cozy and seemingly undisturbed.

He pulled her inside and shut the door. "Don't move while I clear the house."

She saluted and folded her hands in front of her.

With Raz at his side, they cleared the small two-bedroom bungalow. The sweep was quick, not allowing time to really take in her dwelling, but he was left with the impression of a comfortable and feminine home.

He returned to the small living room with the couch facing a picture window looking out over the beach and ocean. "All clear."

She visibly relaxed and dropped her purse on the end table next to the couch.

His phone rang. The caller ID announced the caller was Jeremy. His best friend and his boss. "It's your brother."

She paused. "Put it on speaker, please."

Nodding, he pressed the button. "Chief, you're on with me and Julia."

"Where are you?" Jeremy asked.

"Your sister's. She needed to freshen up and grab some clothes to go to your parents'."

A chuckle met his answer. "And I would imagine she talked you into stopping at the sanctuary, too."

Julia scoffed. "Bah."

Tarren grinned. "She's your sister, what do you think?"

"Always the princess, that one," Jeremy said, with good humor.

Rolling her eyes, Julia said, "Does that make you a prince?"

"Of course," Jeremy replied. "Prince Charming at your service."

Julia barked out a laugh. Tarren joined her.

There had been some sibling rivalry and jealousy through the years. Tarren was glad to see that both Jeremy and Julia had outgrown their differences.

"We'll be heading to your parents' shortly," Tarren told him.

"Good. I'll meet you there later. The bomb tech said the device was sophisticated. Something used by the cartels."

Julia gasped.

The news forced the breath from Tarren's lungs. "Had the cartel planned to hold Amber for ransom? The alternative would be human trafficking." Tarren really didn't want that to be the case.

"Hard to say," Jeremy replied in a grim tone. "I've been in contact with the FBI, DEA and ATF. They ID'd the would-be kidnapper. Gomez Iglesias. An enforcer for the Rio Diablo Cartel."

"Julia and Amber didn't say there was anyone with him," Tarren pointed out. Julia nodded to confirm. "Do you think he was acting alone?"

"Doubtful," Jeremy replied. "Where there's one cockroach there are more. Federal agents will be coming to the island and setting up shop."

Tarren's stomach clenched. "They're taking over?"

"I invited them for a joint investigation," Jeremy replied. "But it will be our job to keep Julia safe. I won't trust anyone else with my baby sister."

Seeing the way Julia's face drained of color made Tarren regret letting her hear this conversation.

"You know I will do everything in my power to keep her safe," Tarren said.

"You're the best," Jeremy said. "Oh, and I contacted the police chief in the Lynns' hometown. He'll make sure to keep Amber and her family protected."

"Good to know. We'll see you later." Tarren hung up.

"What do you know about this Rio Diablo Cartel?" Julia asked.

Raz moved to nudge Julia, offering her comfort. She bent to give Raz a hug, then straightened.

Tarren's mouth went dry. He wanted a hug. He cleared his throat in an effort to chase away the inappropriate thought, and said, "The cartel is out of Mexico City." He contemplated keeping what he knew of the cartel from her but then decided she needed to know what they were up against. "The Rio Diablo has a reputation for cutting down those who oppose them in ways that make any horror flick you could ever imagine seem tame."

Julia's hands gripped the back of the couch.

Tarren moved quickly, folding her in his arms. "You have nothing to worry about. Raz and I will protect you with our lives."

She splayed her hands on his chest and met his gaze. Her blue eyes sparked with fire. "I know I should be afraid, but I'm mad. This is our island. Our home. We can't let some cartel invade our shores. We must stop them."

Tarren stared in amazement at the warrior woman within his arms. She was magnificent. And it took all his willpower to not dip his head and kiss her.

Instead, he released her and stepped back. "That's the plan. But you will have no part in it."

She tossed her hair. "We'll see about that."

He had a sinking feeling in the pit of his gut that she wasn't going to be so easy to protect. Strong-willed, stubborn and beautiful was a potent combination that was going to test all of his skills.

But he was up for the challenge.

Raz let out a series of ferocious barks, his gaze riveted to the large picture window overlooking the ocean.

On the shore, headed for Julia's house, were several men carrying automatic weapons. Weapons aimed directly at the window.

FOUR

Adrenaline flooded Tarren's veins. He launched himself at Julia, taking her to the floor. "Down!"

A barrage of gunfire peppered the house, the noise deafening. The beachside window exploded in a rain of glass, reaching even where they hid behind the couch.

Tarren grabbed Raz by the vest and pulled him closer. When he took his hand away, there was blood smeared across his palm. Heart pounding, he had no time to check where or how his partner had been injured. He sent up a prayer asking God that Raz's wound wasn't life-threatening.

Bullets whizzed over their heads and glass rained down as the men outside Julia's bungalow continued to spray the house with gunfire. Somehow the Rio Diablo Cartel had discovered Julia's identity and her home address. He had to get Julia and Raz out of the line of fire. He tapped Julia on the shoulder to draw her attention.

She uncurled from the ball she'd tucked herself into enough to lift her head and meet his gaze. Fear shone in the depths of her eyes. His gut clenched.

"When I tell you," he shouted to be sure she heard him, "run to the bathroom and get in the bathtub."

Confusion crossed her face as she shouted back, "What about you? And Raz?"

"We'll be right behind you," he assured her as he unholstered his weapon.

She frowned but nodded and moved to get her feet beneath her while still staying in a crouch.

"On three," he yelled. "One, two, three!"

Tarren popped up from behind the couch and fired back at the men outside as Julia ran in a crouch for the hallway. When she disappeared into the first door on the left, Tarren squatted behind the couch again as another barrage of bullets created damage and chaos.

Beside him, Raz panted, his dark eyes trained on Tarren.

"Sorry, buddy." Tarren scooped the dog into his arms and then ran for the safety of the bathroom with bullets chasing him.

Once inside, he gently set Raz into the tub with Julia. She wrapped her arms around the dog. Raz licked her face.

Tarren turned, then shut and locked the bathroom door, though he knew that wouldn't keep their attackers out. He just needed to buy enough time for Jeremy and the others to arrive.

The gunfire ceased. The silence was unnerving.

Tensing, Tarren braced himself with his left knee on the tile floor and his right knee supporting his hand with the gun aimed at the bathroom door.

A crash reverberated through the house.

The front door had been breached.

Taking calming breaths, Tarren kept his aim steady.

"Julia! Tarren!"

Jeremy. Tarren dropped his chin to his chest. He holstered his weapon and opened the door. Still cautious, he peered around the edge of the doorframe. The house was quickly filling with South Padre police officers with their weapons drawn.

"Are you okay?"

Tarren swiveled to find Jeremy at the other end of the hall, having apparently gone to Julia's room first.

There was no time to give in to the relief coursing through his veins. Tarren answered, "Julia is okay. Raz is injured."

Jeremy pushed past Tarren.

Julia climbed out of the tub and gave her brother a quick hug. "We have to get Raz to the vet."

Tarren slipped around Jeremy and Julia to lift Raz into his arms. Blood smeared the white surface of the tub. Refusing to give up hope, Tarren carried his partner out of the house.

* * *

"I can't stand this." Julia's heart still thundered in her ears as she paced the veterinarian's waiting area.

Her heart ached for Tarren. He sat in the chair, elbows on his knees and his head cradled in his hands. No doubt tormented by the fact his partner was injured. He'd driven them to the local vet, who had whisked Raz into the back the moment they'd arrived. They were both covered in Raz's blood; the sight curled her stomach. Her arms wrapped around her middle, just as she'd wrapped them around Raz in the bathtub. The dog was so brave.

She lifted another plea to God that Raz would be okay. She was amazed neither she nor Tarren had been hit by the flying bullets. She'd had to pick glass out of her hair and from her clothes. She had a few small cuts that weren't more than scratches.

How had Gomez Iglesias and the Rio Diablo Cartel known where she lived? Would she ever feel safe in her home again? Not that there was much left of her house after being riddled with bullets. Learning that a cartel with a horrible name was running some kind of criminal activity on South Padre Island set her nerves jumping and her blood boiling.

What had they intended to do with Amber? Various scenarios played across her mind, and she shuddered, thankful that she'd been there to save the young teen.

Just as she was thankful Tarren had been there at the house with her, though her heart ached because poor Raz had paid a price for protecting her.

Tarren lifted his head. "Dr. Martin is the best. He's been tending to Raz since I brought him home from the breeder."

Appreciating that he was trying to reassure her, she moved to sit beside him. She took his hand. "I'm so sorry this happened."

He squeezed her hand. "Don't you dare feel guilty. This is not on you."

She knew that logically, but it still didn't ease the pain of knowing Raz was hurt because of her.

Time ticked and her nerves stretched. Anxiety crawled up her throat.

The veterinarian, a tall man with kind blue eyes and gray hair, walked through the swinging doors.

Tarren stood, raising her with him. She clung to his hand, her pulse beating with dread.

"Good news," Dr. Martin said with a smile. "He had a piece of glass in his shoulder. We cleaned and dressed the wound. He'll need to take it easy for a day or two, but he'll recover fully."

Julia let out a breath of relief and her knees turned to jelly. If she hadn't been clinging to Tarren's hand, she'd have sunk to the floor.

Tarren shook the doctor's hand with his free hand. "Thank you. I don't know what I would've done if—"

"Raz is a tough boy," Dr. Martin said. "We've sedated him. I'd like to keep him overnight just to make sure that the wound doesn't become infected."

"Sure. Of course." Tarren took a shuddering breath. "I'll be back first thing in the morning to pick him up."

Outside the vet's office, three police cruisers waited next to Tarren's truck. He stepped over to talk with one of the officers before moving to his vehicle. He opened the passenger door and she climbed in.

The severity of the situation made the fine hairs on her arms rise.

A cartel, Rio Diablo, wanted her dead.

She itched to get on the computer and discover who these people were and what they were into. Her guess was human trafficking. But were they also into drugs and illegal weapons? Had they always been operating on the island? Or was this something new?

Tarren jumped into the driver's seat, waved that he was ready to leave at the other officers and headed the vehicle down the street with the police cruisers pulling in behind to follow. They approached town but instead of turning right, which would take them farther away from the city toward the more residential area where few tourists ventured, he turned left heading down Padre Island Boulevard.

"I thought you were taking me to my parents?"

"We'll get there," he said, his voice terse.

Something in his posture and the way his gaze kept darting to the rearview mirror had her alarm sensors going off. "What's wrong?"

"Hopefully, nothing."

He reached for the radio attached to his uniformed shoulder. He thumbed the mic. "Be advised," he said into the device. "A silver sedan with missing plates is following my escort."

The dispatcher's tinny voice filled the cab. "Got it. Relaying message."

Julia twisted in her seat but all she could see were the three South Padre police cruisers.

Tarren took a sharp right turn and then another sharp right turn.

She kept an eye on the side-view mirror and caught a glimpse of the sedan with the missing license plate. "How can you be sure they're following us?"

"They circled the block with us," he said.

Behind them, the three police cruisers peeled off, going in various directions, seemingly leaving her and Tarren unprotected.

"Where are they going?" Julia gripped the door handle and lifted a quick prayer. "You can't take me to my parents if we're being followed."

"Agreed," he said. "Which is why we're headed to the police station."

As they approached the turn that would take them down the alley behind the police station, sirens split the air as the three police cruisers attempted to box in the sedan.

The sedan sped up and did a 180 turn in the middle of the street, barely missing the police cars before racing down a side street with the three cruisers chasing after it.

Julia lost sight of the sedan in the side-view mirror. "The driver's going to cause an accident."

"I'm sure that's the least of his worries." Tarren pulled into the parking lot underneath the police station building. Behind them, the gate rattled down, closing them into the underground parking.

Julia let out a breath. "What's the plan?"

"We're going to hang out here for a bit, then we'll head to your parents," he told her.

Julia shook her head, stomach roiling. "No way. I don't want my parents involved in this."

Warm approval shone in Tarren's gaze. "I agree. Maybe you and your parents could leave the island."

Indignation flared bright within her chest like a flare. "I'm not leaving," she said. "It's nesting season. I'm not letting these bad actors run me off. This island is not that big. Amber's attacker—"

"Gomez Iglesias," Tarren supplied.

"Yeah, him," Julia said. "He can't be that hard to find."

Tarren cocked an eyebrow. "When someone doesn't want to be found, they can make the search difficult."

From over Tarren's shoulder, Julia caught sight of her brother exiting the elevator and stalking toward the SUV where she and Tarren sat.

"Here's Jeremy." She reached for the door handle.

"Let me have a minute with him," Tarren said as he hopped out of the vehicle.

She could hear the two men talking but couldn't make out the words. Hating to be left out of the conversation since it revolved around her, she opened the passenger door and jumped out.

She rounded the end of the SUV to find both men glaring at her. "What?"

"You're such a pill," Jeremy stated.

Not sure what she did to deserve that moniker today, she glared right back at her brother. "You're discussing my fate. I'd like to be in on the conversation."

"I agree that you shouldn't go near Mom and Dad," Jeremy said. "I'll suggest they go visit Aunt Freda in Massachusetts."

"Good idea," Julia said. "Except you might call Aunt Freda and ask her to invite them."

Jeremy rubbed his chin. "I think the request should come from you since you're her favorite."

"Hardly," she said, not sure why he had to go there. "But I'll call her."

Tarren cleared his throat. "Let's take this party inside."

They gathered in the elevator and rode up to the main floor. Once they were ensconced in Jeremy's office, Jeremy pushed his landline phone toward her. "Make the call."

Baring her teeth at his high-handedness, she reached into her pocket to grab her cell phone and brought up Aunt Freda's number. It didn't take much convincing to get her mom's sister to extend an invitation to her parents for a visit.

"You should go with them," Tarren said when she'd hung up.

"And what happens if this cartel follows me to Massachusetts? You two won't be there to protect me, Mom, Dad and Aunt Freda. I should stay here where I have you two, correct?"

Tarren and Jeremy shared a concerned look that had Julia's heart thumping. No way was she leaving the island. The whole point of sending her parents to Aunt Freda's was to protect them.

"You better call Mom and Dad and let them know you're okay," Jeremy said. "Afterward, we'll discuss the logistics of you staying on the island until we get Gomez Iglesias."

Satisfied she wouldn't have to battle the issue with her brother and Tarren, she dialed her parents while Jeremy and Tarren left the office.

Mom and Dad both got on the line. They were understandably upset. But thankful their daughter was safe.

"I just got off the phone with Freda, she wants us to come for a visit," Mom said. "Why don't you join us? After this nasty business, you could use some time away."

Wincing, Julia said, "Mom, you know it's nesting season. You and Dad go, have a good time. I'll be fine. Jeremy and Tarren will make sure I'm safe."

"Is your brother there?" Dad asked.

Tucking in her chin, she made a face. "Somewhere around here. I'll have to find him and have him call you back."

After hanging up, she walked past the dispatch operator's booth and into what Jeremy referred to as the situation room. There were monitors on the wall showing various locations on the island. A large table sat in the middle of the room. Laptops were set up on all four sides. Jeremy and Tarren were both on a laptop.

Jeremy glanced up as she approached. "You shouldn't be back here. I'd like you to wait in my office."

"And I'd like to go about living my life without fear," she quipped. "But I guess neither of us is going to get our wish today, now, are we?"

Jeremy frowned and went back to looking at the laptop.

A snicker from Tarren drew Julia's attention.

"Something funny you want to share?" she asked.

Tarren's grin did funny things to her insides.

"You two bickering reminds me of the old days."

"Glad you find me entertaining," Julia said, crossing her arms over her chest.

Tarren arched an eyebrow. "You're not offended."

She narrowed her gaze. "How do you know?"

"Because Julia Hamilton gives as good as she gets," Tarren said.

Julia's arms dropped to her sides. That may have been true once. But ever since her breakup, she'd questioned everything she believed about herself and about the world. She shifted her attention to Jeremy and held out her phone. "Call Dad."

Jeremy sat back and took the phone. He dialed and waited. "Hey, Dad. Yep. I will. I promise. Okay. Have fun."

He hung up and handed the phone back. "They're leaving in the morning."

Julia was happy that they decided to go. But she needed to figure out what she was going to do now.

"Guess I'm bunking with you?" she said to Jeremy.

However, the thought did not appeal. He lived in a cracker-box studio apartment over the bakery. There was barely enough room for him, let alone her.

"Looks like," Jeremy said, his focus back on his laptop.

"I have a better solution," Tarren piped in. "You both stay with me at my house."

Touched by the offer, she said, "And where do you live?"

She fully expected him to say he lived in another cracker-box studio apartment down the hall from her brother. The two had been inseparable as kids and still seemed to be.

"The same house I grew up in," Tarren said.

Surprised and intrigued, Julia considered his offer. In all the years she'd known Tarren, she'd never been inside his childhood home. He'd always kept her out. Only Jeremy was allowed inside. Her mother had said it was because Tarren was embarrassed by his mother. Julia never understood and had thought it was a lame excuse. Tarren just hadn't wanted his best friend's little sister in his space. But now he was inviting her in.

"Seems like a reasonable plan of action," she said.

As long as she remembered to keep her childhood crush from resurfacing, she'd be safe, ensconced in Tarren's home.

Tarren's heartbeat was in his throat as he pulled into the garage of his childhood home. He ushered Julia to the door leading to the kitchen. Jeremy had stayed at the station and would join them later in the evening.

Julia gestured to the various sports equipment hanging from the garage ceiling. "A paddleboard, surfboard, bicycle and kayak," she said. "I never realized you were so sporty."

He shrugged while fitting his key into the lock and pushing the door open.

"I like to keep active when I'm not on duty."

"Does Raz go with you on your adventures?"

"Of course." Tarren already missed his partner. "He's my constant companion."

He stepped into the kitchen and allowed her to ease past him. He couldn't remember the last time he'd had a female in his home. He'd never had Julia here. He'd never wanted her to know about his mother. But Mom was long gone now and he'd made the home his.

Quickly closing the drapes, he said, "Help yourself to anything you need."

"I'd really love to shower," she said. "But I don't have any clothes to change into."

"I'm sure I can find something for you to wear until we can get you your things." He headed down the hall, aware of her close behind him. He opened the door to the room that had been his haven as a kid. Now, the room had a queen-size bed for guests, not that he had anyone visit. An empty dresser and a bedside table with a lamp he'd found at a garage sale completed the room. "You'll sleep here. Jeremy will have to take the couch."

"Oh, he'll love that," Julia said with a chuckle.

"It's a pullout and pretty comfortable," Tarren replied. "I bought it new last year."

"Okay." Julia stepped into the bedroom. "This is lovely."

"It used to be mine, but after my mom passed, I moved into the master suite." He wasn't sure why he was telling her this.

Compassion shone in her bright eyes. "I was sorry to hear of her passing. I sent you a card."

"I received it." The card still sat on his dresser.

"Can I ask what she died from?"

The question raked through Tarren like talons. To busy his hands, he went to the closet where he had a few boxes of old clothes stashed away. "Alcohol-related liver disease."

"That's so sad."

Tarren grabbed a pair of sweatpants from his high school track days and a sweatshirt with the high school logo on the front. Handing them to her, he said, "The guest bath is across the hall. There are towels under the sink. Tomorrow I'll go back to your place and see if anything is salvageable."

Holding the clothes to her chest, she said, "I only met your mother once when she came to our house looking for you. I didn't realize until much later that she was intoxicated. I take it she was a heavy drinker."

Tarren swallowed the residual anger he harbored toward his mother. "She was. Nothing I said or did motivated her to quit. Even when her liver was shutting down, she wouldn't give up drinking. Too addicted."

"Is that why you kept everyone, aside from Jeremy, at a distance?"

"I was ashamed of my mom," he admitted. "It took me years of counseling to understand her drinking was her way of coping with her pain. And that I wasn't the cause."

Julia moved to place a hand on his arm. "That hurts my heart. I wished I'd known you were suffering."

He covered her hand with his. "I didn't want anyone's pity. And there was nothing you, or anyone else, could have done to change the situation."

"Still. I wish you'd have trusted me with your secret." She released his arm and stepped back. "But I understand. I'm only Jeremy's little sister."

He wanted to tell her she was more than that to him but decided it was better to keep up a wall of distance between them. For both their sakes.

FIVE

The next morning, after a restless night's sleep filled with phantom gunfire and images of Raz and Tarren hurt, Julia was ready to start a new day. Wearing a pair of old sweats from Tarren's high school days, she tiptoed across the hall to the bathroom.

On the sink counter, she found the clothes she'd been wearing the day before already washed and dried, though there were dark stains from Raz's blood, and neatly folded. Her heart gave a little thump. Tarren. No way would it have occurred to her brother to do this kindness for her.

Jeremy had arrived last night with a large pizza and immediately the two guys fell into the old habit of watching sports on TV and riffing on each other.

The old Julia would have inserted herself in their enjoyment, asking questions, making comments and doing everything she could to gain their attention.

But she wasn't that woman anymore. Now she

second-guessed every decision and every inter-
action. Was she as needy as Bryce had accused
her of?

Not sure she wanted to know the answer, she'd
excused herself with a slice of pizza and hid away
in the guest bedroom. She'd tried to read the
thriller novel she had found in the drawer of the
nightstand, but the book hadn't kept her attention. Maybe because she'd lived through her own
little thriller scenario earlier in the day.

Sleep proved elusive as she tossed and turned.
At one point, when she'd gotten up to use the re-
stroom, the sound of her brother snoring in the
living room broke the silence. A sound she did
not miss from living in the same house with him.

And now, here she stood in the bathroom staring at her freshly laundered garments and fighting back tears.

Tarren had probably taken care of his mother
more than she had taken care of him. Empathy
flooded Julia's chest. All these years Tarren had
suffered in silence. She wondered if her parents
had known that his mother had been an alcoholic.

Of course, Jeremy must have known and kept
Tarren's secret. She imagined the reason the two
boys chose to stay silent was so that child protective services wouldn't come in and take Tarren away.

The very thought of not having grown up with
Tarren in her life made Julia's stomach quiver

with an unfamiliar sensation. She chalked it up to sympathy and her dislike of change.

She hurt for Tarren and all that he must have endured. As memories surfaced, she recalled times when there was an aura of sadness and maybe even desperation surrounding him. Times when he'd arrive at their house in the same clothes as he'd worn the day before and days the dark circles under his eyes made him look a bit haunted.

She'd been too young to understand the nuances or read the signs that something was amiss in his life. Still, she couldn't stop the prick of pain because he hadn't confided in her. But that wasn't really fair. To him, she was nothing more than a nuisance—just his best friend's annoying little sister.

She bowed her head and lifted a prayer. "Lord, how do I proceed? I don't want to be mad at Tarren. I don't want to pity him, either. I want to be of help."

Though to be honest, he didn't need her help. He'd made such a great life for himself. He was a respected officer and an admirable man. *Grace.* The word reverberated through her like a soft breeze.

Of course she could extend grace to Tarren.

But to herself?

No. She'd been a fool to trust the wrong man. She'd been a fool to believe the lies that had rolled so easily off Bryce's tongue. He'd made her feel like she was the most important person in the world. He'd deceived her. Then he'd destroyed her. Belittling her with accusations that had left jagged wounds.

She gave herself a shake to dislodge the thoughts of Bryce and the past.

She needed to focus on the now. On staying alive. On helping Tarren and Jeremy find Gomez Iglesias.

She wasn't arrogant enough to think she could actually help in any viable way. But she could do some research if her laptop survived the destruction caused by the armed men who'd sprayed her place with bullets. She shuddered at the memory and quickly changed into her own clothes. Thankfully, her brother had brought her purse to her last night. She slung the strap over her shoulder and left the room.

She found Tarren and Jeremy in the kitchen drinking coffee.

"Good morning, sunshine," Jeremy said, tipping his cup at her. He was dressed in his police uniform.

"Morning," she replied, looking longingly at the carafe of coffee.

Tarren, dressed in well-worn jeans and a long-sleeved T-shirt, held a mug out to her. "A dash of cream and a dollop of honey."

She couldn't stop the burst of happiness that he'd remembered how she liked her coffee. When she was in high school, Tarren and Jeremy would come home from college, and she'd have coffee with them before her parents got up in the mornings. Those times were special, times when Tarren and Jeremy treated her like an equal.

She took the mug and sipped slowly from the steaming brew, enjoying the dark roast smoothed out by the cream and sweetened by the honey. "Do you think it would be safe now to go to my house so I can pack some bags and see if there's anything usable left?"

Jeremy set his cup down on the counter with a clunk. "You're staying put. I'll go to the house, grab what I can that hasn't been destroyed and bring it back to you."

A protest rose, but she bit the words back. She didn't relish going back to her house yet. "I would appreciate you doing that. I'll make a list of what I need." She turned to Tarren. "Then you and I will go pick up Raz."

Tarren met her gaze. She could see the argument brewing in his eyes.

Before he could say anything, she hurriedly, said, "I'm not staying here by myself. And you promised the doctor you would pick up Raz in the morning. Well, it's morning. You and I will go pick him up." She was not going to be left alone.

"Sis, don't be a pain," Jeremy said. "You'll be fine here by yourself. We'll have a patrolman out front."

She set her coffee mug down carefully and placed her hands on her hips. "So you'll entrust my safety to another officer. Really?"

"All of my officers are top-notch," Jeremy stated, mimicking her stance with his hands on his hips.

She had to admit her brother could be formidable, especially in his uniform. Broad-shouldered, tapered waist and long legs. But she would not be intimidated. She supposed he was handsome with his blue eyes and dark auburn hair. Her friends were always crushing on him and Tarren.

She turned to Tarren, who held up a hand in surrender. Her heart thumped with attraction. He was as tall as her brother, leaner but just as formidable with a grin that tied her up in knots.

"Don't put me in the middle of this," Tarren said.

"Are you afraid to take me with you?" she asked with challenge infused in her tone.

He chuckled. "Like I said yesterday, Julia Hamilton gives as good as she gets. No, I am not afraid to take you with me." He pointed a finger at Jeremy. "He's my best friend, but he's also my boss."

"But he's not my boss," Julia said.

"Come on, Jules," Jeremy said. "Be reasonable."

"I can be very reasonable," she said. "So reasonable that I will go with Tarren to pick up Raz and your police officers can escort us. They got us to the police station yesterday, didn't they?"

Jeremy sighed. "Fine."

She pressed her lips together to suppress the grin wanting to break free.

"Tarren, take her with you to pick up Raz," Jeremy said. "I'll have a couple of patrol officers follow behind." Jeremy headed for the front door. "Check in later."

"Wait! My list."

Jeremy crossed his arms over his chest and waited at the door.

To Tarren, she asked, "Paper and pen?"

He went to a kitchen drawer and produced both. She quickly wrote out what she required and where to find the items.

"Thank you," she said sweetly as Jeremy took the piece of paper.

His mouth lifted on one side as he glanced at the long list. "I'll see you tonight."

After Jeremy left, Julia finished her coffee and rinsed out her mug. "Shall we?"

Tarren shook his head with a wry smile. "You are a force to be reckoned with."

His words wrapped around her, and she wanted to revel in them. But then Bryce's mocking laughter filled her head. "I'm not. I can stand up to my brother. I've been doing it my whole life."

Tarren frowned and cocked his head. "You stand up to me perfectly fine."

"You're like family," she said with a teasing smile.

"And you stood up to Gomez Iglesias," he pointed out. There was no mistaking the pride in his voice. "If you hadn't, who knows what would have happened to Amber."

"I saw someone in trouble and reacted." Doing nothing hadn't been an option. "I did what anyone would have done," she said, needing to downplay the situation and deflect the attention off her.

"Not true," he countered. "Most people would have stood by frozen in fear for themselves. Maybe called for help, but it would have been too late. Or some would have videoed the incident and posted it online."

She made a face. "That's a pretty jaded statement."

He shrugged. "What can I say? In this job, you see the worst of humanity."

"I can only imagine."

"What you did took courage." The soft timbre of his voice shivered through her. "You're a hero."

The moniker didn't sit well. A hero was someone brave and admirable. Someone other than her. She tucked her arm through his, to distract him and herself. "Let's go get your partner."

Tarren pulled into the veterinarian clinic's parking lot and parked. Two South Padre Island police cruisers slid into the spaces on either side of their vehicle. The drive from his house to the clinic had been silent. He couldn't quite find the words to ask what was eating away at Julia. But he could tell there was something. He'd never known her not to be confident. Jeremy hadn't said anything about her life other than she'd broken up with a college boyfriend last year.

Maybe Tarren needed to do a little digging. Not that her past was any of his business. What had happened in her life before she returned home had nothing to do with this case or the reason he was protecting her. Still, he was consumed with a need to know.

While the patrol officers waited outside, Tarren and Julia walked into the vet clinic.

The receptionist gave a wave. "We'll have Raz out to you in a moment. He's such a good boy."

Tarren expected nothing less of his partner. Smart and obedient, that was Raz.

Dr. Martin walked into the waiting area with Raz on a leash. The dog's right shoulder had been shaved and covered by a bandage.

Raz barked a greeting.

Tarren held up a hand, letting the dog know to be patient.

"He's good to go," Dr. Martin said.

"Thank you, Doc." Tarren took the lead from the vet and then knelt on the floor and gave Raz the release signal. Raz climbed into his lap and licked his face.

"Should he be doing that?" Julia asked, concern evident in her voice.

Holding Raz around the middle, Tarren stared up at the vet.

"He'll be fine in a day or two," Dr. Martin replied. "You'll need to keep the wound clean, so it doesn't become infected."

One of the vet techs handed over a bag. "More dressings for the wound and antibiotic cream."

Taking the bag, Tarren stood and thanked Dr. Martin again.

When they were back in the car, Julia said, "I noticed your cupboards are pretty bare. Not to mention you have an expired milk carton and only two eggs left. I'm really not up for more pizza. We need to go to the grocery store on the way back to your place."

"I can have the store deliver," Tarren told her.

"If you think it's wise to have someone you don't know come to your house," she said, her voice filled with a dubious note.

Doubts filled his chest. He didn't want someone coming to the house, knowing where he lived, and possibly discovering that Julia was staying there.

They had their police escort. There was no reason they couldn't stop at the local mini-market. He let the officers escorting them know that they would be making a quick stop. The parking lot wasn't full and they found an empty spot near the door. The two police cruisers pulled up in nearby spaces.

At the entrance, Tarren paused before stepping inside to say to the officers, "You can hang back."

He could only imagine the stir the sight of three officers, Raz with a bandage on his shoulder and a feisty redhead would cause entering the market. The officers waited outside the entrance.

Once inside, Julia pushed the shopping cart while Raz stayed at her side, forcing Tarren to keep up so that the leash wouldn't pull on the dog's harness.

A man wearing a shirt with the market's logo stacked cans of soup on a shelf. He paused to stare at them, his gaze lingering on Julia before he turned away, picked up an empty box and hurried toward the back of the market, disappearing behind a set of swinging doors.

"Let's move this along," Tarren urged, the back of his neck prickling.

"Just a sec." Julia pulled out her phone and typed into the box on a search engine.

Irritation skipped along his skin. "What are you doing?"

"I noticed your recycle bin had a lot of takeout boxes, especially pizza boxes," she said as she scrolled through what appeared to be recipes.

Making a face, he shrugged. "We've already established I'm not much of a cook."

She lifted her gaze to meet his. "You have an electronic multicooker in your cupboard."

The heat of embarrassment made the collar of his shirt too tight. "An impulse buy. I thought I'd try to eat healthy if it were easier."

She arched one auburn brow. "And?"

"I've never used it," he admitted with a resigned sigh. Cooking just wasn't his thing.

"I love mine," she said. "What do you think of...ranch chicken, beef and bean chili, beef teriyaki?"

"Those all sound wonderful, but that seems like a lot of food. Will it keep?"

Pushing the cart down the aisle, she said, "We'll put them in individual containers for the freezer so all you have to do is warm up a meal."

"Julia, you don't have to take care of me."

Pink stained her cheeks. "I know. But I'm going to. Besides, I have a feeling many of those boxes were provided by my brother. This way you both can eat something besides pizza."

Appreciating her thoughtfulness but also a bit uncomfortable with the idea of her preparing meals for him, he said, "Whatever gets us out of here."

After filling the shopping cart, they headed to the checkout stand. In the mirrors above the door aimed strategically to show the back of the grocery store, movement caught Tarren's eye.

Two men filed out of the swinging door at the

back of the market. Both were dressed in black, and their faces were covered by ski masks. Each carried high-powered weapons.

Apparently, word had reached El Diablo that Julia was in the market.

No doubt the squirrelly stock guy who had drawn Tarren's attention had sent out an alert.

Customers screamed and dived for cover as the men advanced toward the front of the store.

Raz growled deep in his throat. Tarren gripped Julia by the elbow and pulled her down behind one of the cash registers.

The cashier stared down at them. "Uh, you can't be back here."

Julia tugged the younger woman to a crouch.

"Do you have an alarm system?" Tarren asked, keeping Julia and Raz tucked low.

The cashier pointed past Julia's head to a button underneath the cash register counter.

Tarren nodded and pushed the silent alarm.

"We don't want to hurt anyone," a heavily accented voice called out. "Just give us the woman."

Over Tarren's dead body would he ever give up Julia.

The sliding entrance doors to the mini-mart swished open and the two South Padre Island police officers who had been waiting outside for Tarren and Julia ran in. The silent alarm had alerted them to the dicey situation.

"Police! Drop your weapons," one of the officers shouted.

Through the mirror's reflection, Tarren noted the two gunmen hesitated. Then one spoke in rapid Spanish before turning tail and running toward the back of the store.

Tarren only caught a couple of the words. But something to the effect of not going to jail. The remaining gunman growled, then turned and raced after his friend.

Jumping to his feet, intent on giving chase, Tarren halted when Julia grabbed his sleeve.

"Stay with us," she pleaded.

The fear in her eyes hit him like a punch to the gut. He remained in place.

The two South Padre Island police officers hurried to Tarren's side.

"Are you hurt?" Officer Carl Anders asked.

Reining in his frustration at being caught unaware, Tarren said, "Go. Get those two."

"On it," the younger officer, Daniel Fielding, said. Both men ran through the store, dodging the customers emerging from where they'd hidden, and disappeared out the back.

Tarren helped Julia to her feet. "We need to get out of here."

"We need to pay for our stuff," she reminded him.

The cashier stood. "I'm sure the manager would be fine if you just take your basket."

Julia pushed past Tarren to round the cashier's desk. "Nonsense. We will pay. Just ring it up quickly, please."

Tarren heaved a sigh and he and Raz moved to stand beside Julia.

The cashier rang up the items and Julia paid before Tarren could reach for his wallet.

The two police officers were standing out front when Tarren and Julia emerged from the mini-mart.

"They got away," Anders stated. "They had a getaway car waiting. We called in the make, model and plate."

Sirens punctuated the air as more South Padre Island police officers arrived on the scene, including Jeremy.

Tarren didn't relish explaining to his boss and friend what had happened.

After hurrying from his car, Jeremy held up a hand. "I got the gist of the situation from Dispatch."

Tarren cocked his head. "I didn't call this in."

"One of the customers in the store called 911," he said. "Plus, the silent alarm and then the *be on the lookout* for the getaway car."

Julia stepped in front of Tarren. "This is my fault. We needed a few things."

Jeremy shrugged. "I can't keep you in a glass case, Julia."

Tarren said, "There was a box boy. I'm positive he's the one who alerted the cartel to our presence."

Jeremy nodded. "Then we'll pick up the kid and question him. You two head back to your place. With your escort. I'll take over here."

Julia hugged her brother. "Thank you, Jeremy."

Tarren met Jeremy's gaze over Julia's head.

Fire lit his boss's eyes. "Promise me you'll keep her safe."

Like he had to ask. "Of course."

Once Julia was settled in Tarren's vehicle, Tarren picked up Raz and set him in the back compartment. Raz lay down with a sigh. Tarren drove them straight to his home with the police escort right on their tail. When they reached the house, he parked the vehicle in the garage and shut the door. "Let me clear the house. Don't move."

He hopped out and made short work of walking through his home to be sure no one waited inside. Nothing was out of place.

Back in the garage, he held out his hand for Julia. She slipped her small, strong hand in his, and a bolt of heat zoomed up his arm. He cleared his throat. "You and Raz go on in, and I'll bring the groceries," he said. "I want to touch base with the officers outside."

He popped open the dog door for Raz. He lifted him out and set him on the floor. "Go with Julia," he instructed the dog.

Raz hesitated, then slowly moved to where Julia waited at the door to the kitchen.

Heading out the back door of the garage, Tarren sent up a quick prayer that he wouldn't fail to keep Julia safe.

SIX

Entering the house shrouded in shadows, it took all of Julia's self-control not to throw open the curtains and let the spring sunshine in. But Tarren had gone to such lengths to make sure no one could see inside that she knew doing so would upset him. They'd both had enough of a scare today.

Worry tumbled through her gut like broken shards of glass. Someone in the store had alerted the cartel to their presence. Unbelievable. The moment Tarren's fingers had gripped her elbow and tucked her into a crouch, she'd begun trembling with fear. Even now, as she made her way to the cupboard in the kitchen to pull out the electronic multicooker, her hands shook, and the lid of the machine rattled.

How had the cartel become so entrenched in South Padre Island that they had spies everywhere? Even the local mini-mart?

She set the cookware on the counter with a *thunk* as a good dose of anger wound through her. How long would this last? She had a life that she was missing out on every second that the cartel had her cowering inside Tarren's home.

At some point, she would have to resume her life. Spring was a busy time at the sanctuary. Turtles would be nesting soon. She had responsibilities. There were school trips where she was scheduled to lecture and fundraising efforts that she'd been arranging. She couldn't stay trapped like an animal in a cage, fearing to step out into the light. That was no way to live.

Taking deep breaths, she scolded herself for her impatience. She had to allow Jeremy and the police department time to catch Gomez Iglesias.

Going about her normal routine right now wasn't an option. She needed to lie low with Tarren and not let the fear win.

A very different type of anxiety wormed its way to the forefront of her mind.

Lying low with Tarren held its own form of danger for her. She couldn't let her guard down and allow the attraction and tender feelings she harbored for Tarren to take root and grow into something she didn't even want to contemplate. Doing so would only set her up for more heartache. She'd suffered enough because of love. She had no intention of suffering again. Ever.

"Here we go." Tarren brought in the bags of groceries and set them on the kitchen table.

She moved to the bags and began unloading the contents. "Ranch chicken or teriyaki beef?"

She held a package of chicken in one hand and beef chunks in the other.

Tarren paused as he stashed a loaf of bread in the cupboard. "Each sounds delicious. Which is easier?"

She shrugged. "They're about the same. Both easy-peasy. Let's do the ranch chicken."

"Works for me." Tarren put a gallon of milk in the fridge. "Let me feed Raz and get him settled, then I'll come help."

"That's not necessary." Affection unfurled in her chest. Had she been trapped with Bryce, he would've gladly left her to her own devices while he spread out on the couch to watch sports. Never once had he offered to help when they'd dated. And she'd kept the fact it bothered her to herself. Which in retrospect had been a mistake.

But now Tarren was offering. Though the kitchen was certainly large enough for them both to move around unimpeded, there was something intimate about cooking with someone else.

"Julia, you do not need to take care of me." Tarren's voice shivered through her. "I want to learn how to make this for myself. I'm sure you'll be a good teacher."

His words soothed her hesitation. This was a teachable moment, nothing more. The attraction and affection that flooded her system was for her friend. The man was willing to put his life in danger to protect her. The least she could do was show him how to make a few delicious meals. "Okay, then."

Resolutely, Julia set everything out on the counter they would need for the ranch chicken. Tarren headed out to feed Raz. She smiled as she listened to Tarren keeping up a one-sided conversation with his partner.

"Here you go, buddy. I know you probably still have a lot of drugs in your system, but that's okay. You need to eat a little bit. I'm going to learn to use that fancy gadget in the kitchen. I'll come check on you in a bit."

Julia brought up the recipe on her phone and started hunting for measuring cups.

Tarren joined her and washed his hands. "What can I do?"

She handed him the packet of chicken. "Dice these into small cubes."

"That I can do," he said.

As she measured out milk into a mixing bowl for the ranch dressing mix, she watched Tarren work. He rolled the sleeves of his shirt up, revealing his muscular forearms sprinkled with dark hair that matched the hair on his head. He worked methodically cutting the chicken with a large chopping knife. If he hadn't said he didn't like to cook, she would never have guessed. He seemed proficient with the instrument.

She plugged the multicooker in and rinsed a cup of rice. When all the ingredients were ready, she stuffed everything into the deep stainless steel appliance, secured the lid, made sure the steam vent was closed and then set the timer. "Now we wait."

Tarren stood close, their shoulders touching. "That's it?"

She blinked slowly as a rush of awareness zinged through her veins. She cleared her throat to reply, "Yep. I told you. Easy-peasy."

"You did." His soft gaze held her enthralled. "Note to self, believe Julia."

A small laugh escaped her but the tension bubbling within her didn't lessen. "Don't let Jeremy hear you say that."

"It will be our secret," he murmured with a smile that set her heart to pounding.

She liked the way the corners of his mouth tipped upward. She'd always thought he had a nice face, symmetrical and angled in all the right places. Her hand itched to trace his stubbled jawline. The sudden and sharp yearning to be held, to be cherished, gripped her lungs and made her dizzy. She swayed slightly toward him, her hands coming up to rest on his chest for balance. His heart beat in an erratic rhythm beneath her palms.

His hands came up to rest lightly on her shoulders. "Julia?"

The way he said her name made her insides melt.

What was she doing? Oh no. No, no, no. She

didn't need anyone to hold her, cherish her or make her melt. Especially not her brother's best friend. Danger lay down that stretch of sand. And she'd learned the hard way emotion could be blown away with the slightest breeze. She stepped back to put distance between them.

"Sorry, I tend to forget to breathe," she said to cover her gaffe.

One of his eyebrows rose. "Breathing is important."

"True." She moved to wash the dishes they'd used. She didn't need to turn her gaze in his direction to know he was watching her.

"I'm going to clean myself up," he said. "I think I got some chicken juice on me."

She laughed. "We wouldn't want that. I'll be fine. Raz will sound an alarm if we need you."

"The TV remote is on the coffee table." He headed out of the kitchen and down the hall, disappearing into his room.

After finishing the cleanup, she sank onto the couch to surf the channels and found nothing to keep her interest. She switched off the TV and tried to relax but her body was wound up. She grew antsy quickly. On the bookcase next to the window, she noticed several large photo albums. And on one of the shelves sat the old Kodak camera that Tarren had constantly carried with him when they were young. She made a note to ask him if he still liked photography.

Needing something to do, she rose to check on the multicooker, but everything was going without a hitch there. She set the dining room table for three, and then cut up some crudités vegetables to go with their ranch chicken and rice. When she was done with those chores, she wandered back into the living room and let her curiosity get the better of her.

She sat on the floor cross-legged and grabbed a photo album. She flipped open the cover. In the scrawling penmanship of a youth, a young Tarren had written "Days in the Life of Tarren." So cute.

She flipped open to the first set of photographs. Baby pictures of Tarren. He'd been a chubby bundle of joy. The images sparked an old longing for a baby of her own, someone to love without conditions. Would that dream ever become a reality? She didn't know and was grateful that during this mess with the cartel, she didn't have the added terror of a child being in jeopardy.

The next few pages of the album had photos of Tarren as a baby with a younger version of his mom and a tall man who she guessed was Tarren's father. She kept turning the pages, watching as Tarren grew from an infant to a toddler to preschool and to grade school. His family life had started out as the type everyone hoped for, then something had gone wrong.

Jeremy had met Tarren in first grade and they became best buddies. Now the photos included

Jeremy and Julia and other students from school and the neighborhood as the photos progressed forward, aging Tarren, Jeremy and Julia. Several of the photos were a surprise.

There were several of her over the years unaware she was the subject of Tarren's camera's focus.

A funny sensation grew in the pit of her stomach. Why would he take pictures of just her?

She turned the pages and found photos of Jeremy, also caught unaware, and then photos of his mother. Her heart ached at one where his mother lay sprawled out on the couch, nearly falling off, with empty alcohol bottles lying beside her. Empathy twisted in her chest.

"Those were dark days."

Julia jumped and slammed the photo album shut. "I'm sorry. I didn't mean to pry. I was just looking for something to do."

He skirted around her and folded his long legs as he sat beside her. "It's okay. You know my mom was a drunk now."

The prick of not being trusted with his secret stung. "Why didn't you ever say anything to me?"

He tilted his head, his gaze searching her face. "What could you have done? You were too young, and I didn't want to rob you of your innocence."

She blinked back the sting of tears. His thoughtfulness was sweet yet made her feel bad at the same time. "Did my parents know?"

He gave a wry smile. "What do you think?"

"They had to have," she decided. "That's why you always were at our house and why my parents were quick to include you in our family vacation adventures."

He reached for another photo album and opened to the pages labeled High School.

"Your parents paid for me to be on the baseball team with Jeremy." He turned the photo album around so she could see the team photos.

Both Jeremy and Tarren looked handsome in their uniforms. She touched the image. "I remember you were really good."

"Not as good as Jeremy," he said. "Jeremy could've gone to the majors."

Sadness descended, crimping her chest. "The tragedy changed everything."

"Yes. Coach Evan's death derailed so many lives."

She traced her finger over the picture of the tall, smiling baseball coach who had also been an English teacher at the high school. Coach Evans had been murdered during Jeremy and Tarren's senior year. His body had been found behind the dugout. Someone had taken a baseball bat to his head. "Did they ever learn who killed him?"

Tarren shook his head. "The case is still open."

He turned the page in the album, and she smiled to see her brother dressed in a powder blue tuxedo with ruffles standing next to a willowy blonde in a sequined gown. "Kara Evans. I wonder whatever happened to her after her father's death."

She and her mother had left town not long after Coach Evans's murder. Their house still stood empty to this day. Julia knew that Mrs. Evans had gardeners and housekeepers to keep the house pristine because she claimed she intended to return after her grieving. But she and Kara never did come back. It had broken Jeremy's heart. As far as she knew, he hadn't had another serious relationship since Kara.

"Jeremy didn't tell you?"

Her curiosity piqued, she said, "Spill, now."

"Kara works for the FBI. She's a profiler."

Julia tucked in her chin. "Wow. All three of you went into law enforcement. What are the odds?"

"High, I would imagine," he said. "The three of us vowed to find out who killed Coach Evans. And the only way to do that..." He trailed off with a shrug.

"I had no idea. I'd always wondered what prompted the two of you to join the police academy." Then a thought occurred to her. "Jeremy and Kara stayed in contact?"

Tarren nodded. "For the first year. But then Kara sent him a Dear John letter."

"I remember." She'd been so angry when her mother had told her about the letter. "Jeremy was devastated. But how do you all know she's with the FBI?"

"Kara has made a name for herself in Washington, DC," he said. "It may seem like we're isolated here on the island, but information is at your fingertips."

Julia barked a laugh. "Did he cyberstalk her?"

Tarren chuckled. "Nothing so nefarious. But we do get updates from the FBI occasionally on various cases. Her name has appeared in more than one document. Plus, she's sort of famous in certain circles. Through her analysis and profiling, she managed to identify a serial killer working his way through the Midwest, which led to an arrest and incarceration."

Julia tried to reconcile her memory of the gregarious and spunky Kara to someone who'd hunt serial killers. Her father's death had a serious impact. Julia shuddered.

The beeping of the multicooker alerted her that their dinner was ready. They returned the photo albums and Tarren rose, offering his hand to her. She clung to him as he lifted her to her feet. For a moment, they stood there with hands clasped and their gazes locked. The dizzy, heady sensation rushed through her again.

As distractions from her situation went, Tarren was a good one. Learning this new information about him filled her with a deep sense of understanding and something more, something tender that seemed to flit at the edge of her consciousness. The air seemed to crack around them. She wanted to lean in, to offer comfort and take comfort. But doing so could cost her in so many ways. A slice of fear cut through the mesmerizing grip he had on her.

She broke the silence stretching between them by asking, "Do you still take pictures?"

He released her hand. "I do. Later, I'll show you some of my most recent work."

"I'd like that."

The sound of the doorknob jingling had them both whipping around to face the front door. Raz rose and sniffed along the doorjamb, then walked away.

"It's your brother," Tarren said, heading over to open the door and allowing Jeremy entrance.

Shaking off the attraction zinging through her veins, Julia hurried into the kitchen to dish up their meal.

"We did good." Tarren smiled his appreciation at Julia. He'd enjoyed helping her cook the meal and it was as easy as she had claimed. The flavors of the ranch chicken were delicious. Better than any takeout he could have ordered.

"Who knew you could cook." Jeremy ate his last bite.

"It's easy-peasy," Tarren quipped, then met Julia's gaze. He liked the way her skin flushed with a pink hue. Despite his upset at knowing the cartel had spies in town, Tarren had enjoyed the afternoon cooking with Julia and then sharing with her the photo albums. He hadn't cracked them open in years. Going down memory lane usually made him depressed. But today not so much. And it was because of Julia.

His heart beat a little fast still. He'd come close to kissing her. Twice. Once in the kitchen when she had stared out at him with such trusting eyes. The dreamy expression on her face had made him consider, perhaps, she was feeling the same attraction pulling at him.

Then again, right before Jeremy arrived. There had been a moment when he'd almost given in to the temptation of her lips. That wouldn't be a good idea. Julia was off-limits. She was his to protect. His best friend's little sister. And his friend in her own right.

He would never do anything to jeopardize his relationships with the Hamilton family.

He needed to keep Julia in the friend zone.

As long as he could remember he'd always liked Julia and had known she would grow into a beauty one day. And a beauty she was. Not only on the outside but inside. She was brave, kind and smart. Independent, yet vulnerable. The kind of woman who deserves better than him.

Needing to redirect his thoughts, Tarren asked

Jeremy, "Did you interview the kid from the mini-mart?"

"We did," Jeremy said with satisfaction as he leaned back in his chair. "The kid caved like a house of cards. It seems his cousin runs with a rough crowd. The cousin put out the word to be on the lookout for Julia. So, when he saw you two in the store, he called his cousin."

Noting the hard expression on his friend's face, Tarren said, "I hope you have the cousin in custody."

"We do. But we can't prove he was there. He lawyered up after claiming he'd just passed on the information and was promised money. We can hold him for the next twenty-four hours without charging him."

Julia splayed her hands on the table as if to steady herself. "So... The cartel put a bounty on my head."

SEVEN

Tarren stared at Julia. Her stark, ominous words reverberated through the air.

The cartel put a bounty on my head.

Meeting Jeremy's fierce gaze, Tarren drew in a sharp breath as grimness settled in his chest.

He'd known when Gomez Iglesias blew up her truck that the man was willing to kill to protect himself. And when masked men riddled her home with bullets and came after her in the mini-market, Tarren realized just how much danger Julia was in, but he hadn't anticipated she'd come to the same conclusion. The Rio Diablo Cartel had a hit out on Julia.

She shrugged. "I watch TV. Real-crime stories, not to mention crime dramas. They know I can identify a member of the cartel." A visible shiver ran over her limbs, and she wrapped her arms around her middle as if to keep from falling apart. "He must be pretty important for them to be going to so much trouble to silence me."

"Agreed. Gomez isn't just some foot soldier."

Acid burned in Tarren's gut, making the delicious meal turn sour.

Jeremy slapped his palm on the table. "I blame Maxwell for this mess. He should never have put your face on camera. Reporters make things worse, not better."

Julia waved away his words. "He's doing his job. If it hadn't been him it would have been somebody else."

Tarren watched Julia closely. She tried to hide the fear lurking in the depths of her pretty eyes, but he could tell the conversation was upsetting to her. It upset him, as well. But she was safe here with him. He wouldn't let anyone get to her.

Jeremy's phone rang and he excused himself to take the call.

Tension dogged Tarren as he helped Julia clear away the dishes and clean up the mess in the kitchen.

By the time Jeremy joined them, they were done.

Julia swatted at her brother with a dish towel. "Figures your call would take the exact amount of time it took us to do the dishes."

Jeremy dodged her with his hands held up and his palms out. "Whoa. Take it easy, sis."

Though the teasing between siblings was familiar, Tarren could tell neither was in a jovial mood.

"News?" Tarren prompted.

"The FBI will be here by tomorrow, end of the day," Jeremy replied.

Concerned and curious if Jeremy's ex, Kara, would be coming, Tarren asked, "Do you think—"

Jeremy cut him off. "No."

Julia's gaze bounced between them. "I understand Kara works for the FBI."

"She does." Jeremy stared at Tarren with an accusatory glare.

Spreading his hands, Tarren said, "She asked about her."

Blowing out a breath that was clearly filled with frustration, Jeremy said, "Field agents and a SAC will be coming."

Julia made a face. "A sack?"

"S.A.C. A special agent in charge who will oversee the agents and work with me on the investigation."

"Ah." Julia tilted her head. "What are they going to be able to do that you all can't?"

Tarren didn't envy his friend the scrutiny that would come from the whole community. Having the Feds involved meant more red tape and more chaos but it also meant more boots on the ground searching for Gomez. Which meant Julia would be safe that much sooner. "The Feds have more resources than our department."

"True," Jeremy confirmed. "As much as I want this cartel dismantled and brought to justice, there are other crimes and issues our department has to deal with every day. We're stretched thin at the moment."

Julia piped up with, "And it's the beginning of tourist season. People come from all over to view the turtle nests and in two months the hatchings. So I see how more help would be appreciated."

"We could use another K9." Tarren and Raz were sometimes needed in multiple places at once. And with Raz out of commission for a few days and Tarren on guard duty, a duty he wouldn't hand off for anything, the island wasn't as well protected as it could be.

"On the wish list," Jeremy said, as he had many times before.

"Hmm, when this is over, I'm going to talk to Dad," Julia said.

Jeremy made a face. "Not a good idea. He may sit on the city council, but he can't show favoritism to the department. All of the island's emergency services have needs."

Tarren could see the wheels turning behind Julia's gaze. He liked that she wanted to help. She'd always been a go-getter. Fearless even. Thinking back on some of the antics he and Jeremy got her into as kids made him wonder how they'd all survived intact.

Julia hung back in the kitchen as Tarren and Jeremy headed into the living room. A few moments later, the TV came on to a sports channel. To busy herself and ease the anxious flutters taking flight in her stomach, she perused the cupboards, looking for ingredients to make something. Anything.

Thankfully, Tarren had all the necessary fixings to make cookie dough. She checked the spice cupboard and found cinnamon. Snickerdoodles would do the trick.

She squared her shoulders, set the oven to heat and went to work measuring out the ingredients. She would be strong. No way would she give in to terror and anxiety. She would not let the stress and fear get the better of her. Though her attempt to lighten the mood earlier hadn't really done the job. She was both frustrated and terrified by the thought of being in the crosshairs of a deadly cartel.

But honestly, she wouldn't change anything. If she hadn't been there on the beach at the exact moment she had been, Amber would be gone. That was unacceptable.

She mulled over the fact the FBI was coming to town. The news both unsettled her and gave her hope. Maybe the Feds would be able to rid the island of the cartel. It wasn't that she didn't believe in her brother or the South Padre Island Police force. But Jeremy had said the department was stretched thin. They needed more help.

A shiver of dread and unease prickled her skin knowing this situation warranted federal agents coming to town. This was a much bigger deal than she had realized.

Once the cookie dough was ready, she made round balls and rolled them in a mix of cinnamon and sugar before putting them on a cookie tray lined with parchment paper she'd found in a drawer. She used the bottom of a small glass to flatten the cookie balls and then popped the tray into the heated oven. Then she made another batch on a second cookie sheet and set it aside to wait its turn to go into the oven.

She supposed that's what she was going to have to do, wait out the situation and try to make the most of the time in Tarren's house. What choice did she have?

Being upset and allowing the fear to take hold wouldn't do her, or anyone, any good. This was a situation that was out of her control. At least she and Tarren had bought enough ingredients to make several savory dishes over the next few days.

Oh, she hoped it wasn't going to be more than a few days. Living in isolation with Tarren as her companion was going to tax every ounce of her resolve not to let her old feelings surface and let new adult emotions grow.

From the living room, the ruckus of the guys cheering brought back memories of other times when they watched their games. Apparently, their team was winning. Yay for them. At least they weren't letting the circumstances dampen their love of sports.

The timer beeped on the cookies. Finding a set of oven mitts, she moved the tray out, set it on the stove and slid the next tray of flattened snickerdoodles into the oven. After placing the warm cookies on a large plate and pouring out three glasses of milk, she headed to the living room with her bounty just like she used to do when they were kids. Some habits never died.

As soon as she walked into the living room, balancing three glasses of milk and the cookie plate, Tarren jumped up and moved quickly to aid her. He'd always been polite and helpful.

He relieved her of the cookie plate. "I wondered what you were doing in there."

"Need to stay busy," she confessed.

His understanding smile unfurled ribbons of affection through her.

He set the cookie plate on the coffee table.

Jeremy immediately grabbed one and popped it into his mouth. "Woooo." He fanned his mouth. "Hot."

Julia rolled her eyes. Her brother never changed. "They just came out of the oven."

He swallowed and glared at her. "You could've said so."

She made a face. "You didn't give me a chance." She shoved a glass of milk at him.

He drank down half of the milk in one gulp.

Tarren's gaze made her flush with embarrassment. Why did she always revert to her thirteen-year-old self around her brother?

Unable to meet Tarren's eyes, she handed him a glass.

"Thank you." His hand wrapped around hers, holding both her and the glass in place. "You really didn't have to. But I do appreciate you taking such very good care of us."

For some reason, his words brought tears to the back of her eyes. Taking care of others was a part of her DNA. Whether it was turtles, humans or any other animal. But knowing that Tarren understood her, and appreciated this trait, touched her deeply.

The zing of attraction and longing zapped her strength. Some part of her acknowledged these feelings running rampant through her system weren't just residual from her teenage self. No, her adult self really liked Tarren, a lot. She could easily find herself traveling down a road she shouldn't.

The ding of the oven alerted her that the next batch of cookies was ready, and she took the opportunity to flee the living room. Just as she got into the kitchen, a series of Raz's barks sent fear ricocheting through her system and rerouted her back to the living room to find Tarren and Jeremy both had drawn their weapons.

Raz barked at the front door, and then he

moved along the walls as if following someone creeping about the house outside.

A shiver of dread rushed over her limbs. "What's hap—" She broke off as Tarren put a finger to his lips indicating for her to be quiet.

Her brother started toward the back door. Tarren held up a hand. "Let me and Raz. Stay with your sister."

A flash of indecision marched over Jeremy's face before he nodded and moved to take Julia's elbow, tugging her down the hall.

"But what about Tarren?" A new kind of fear raced through her veins. Tarren was in danger. What if something happened to him? "You should go with him."

"My job is to protect you. Trust Tarren and Raz," Jeremy said. "I do."

Her heart jammed in her throat. They'd been found at Tarren's house. How? Worry tore through her gut. As Jeremy called for backup, she lifted a whispered prayer. *Please, Lord, please keep Tarren and Raz safe.*

Tarren clipped on a short lead to Raz's collar as they slipped out the side door of the garage. Raz's barking had long ceased. The dog understood they were working now. It was time to go hunting.

They moved along the side of the house to the front where the darkness was only broken by the moon's glow. Someone had unscrewed the light over the front door. His heart rate revved in high gear. Adrenaline flooded his veins. With Raz at his side, they moved cautiously around the corner of the house and slowly worked their way toward the backyard.

Deep shadows created by the moon filtering through the trees played along the sides of the house, generating shapes that unnerved Tarren. Was one of the inky patterns dancing on the wall a human?

The side gate stood open. Wary of intruders, Tarren kept Raz close as they entered the dark backyard. Again, someone had unscrewed the deck light near the back door. Squatting down, he unhooked Raz from the lead and then whispered into the dog's ear, "Find."

The dog took off. Within seconds Raz found the perpetrator hunkered down on the other side of the deck.

A deep masculine voice swore in a mix of English and Spanish, mixing with Raz's snarls.

Tarren hurried after his partner and flipped on his flashlight in time to see Raz jump up and take a huge bite out of the guy's jacket. The man wore a black mask. He and Raz tussled, the man trying unsuccessfully to dislodge Raz.

"Police," Tarren yelled to identify himself to the assailant. Then Tarren gave the "Out" command for Raz to release his hold on the man's jacket. Raz immediately disengaged but stood growling at the intruder, ready to pounce again if the man tried to escape.

The scuff of a shoe behind Tarren alerted him at the same moment that Raz shifted and let out another series of barks before charging forward.

Tarren twisted just as something hard came down squarely on his right shoulder, knocking him to his knees.

Pain from the hit weakened his grip on his weapon but he managed to keep hold of it. He struggled to regain his footing. Raz barked and growled at the second intruder, but the man kept the dog at bay by swinging a large baseball bat in an arc.

The sound of sirens drawing closer was a welcome noise.

"Let's get out of here," one of the two assailants shouted. The two men ran into the darkness.

Raz gave chase. Fearing for his partner, Tarren whistled. Within seconds, the dog had given up the chase and returned to Tarren's side. Somewhere down the block, the sound of an engine turning over and tires squealing on the pavement alerted Tarren that the assailants had escaped.

Julia. Her name reverberated through Tarren's head as he got himself to his feet. He needed to make sure she and Jeremy were okay. Had more intruders breached the house while he was outside?

He stumbled up the stairs to the back sliding door and pounded on the glass. "It's me. Tarren."

Jeremy pushed aside the curtain and then opened the slider.

Unable to lift his arm, Tarren said, "Take the gun."

Quickly and carefully, Jeremy relieved Tarren of his service weapon and tucked it into the back of his waistband. "What happened?"

"You're hurt!" Julia pushed past Jeremy.

"Slightly," Tarren muttered as he allowed the other two to help him to the dining room table. His shoulder and arm throbbed. "There were two of them. Raz took a chunk of one guy's jacket. But they got away. They had a car stashed down the street." What must Julia think of him to let himself get assaulted?

"You need to go to the hospital," Julia insisted.

Tarren waved off her words. "I've had worse."

Jeremy shut and locked the sliding door. "Let's take a look. If I think you need medical attention, you'll get medical attention."

Tarren nodded. He would trust Jeremy's assessment because he wouldn't send him to the doctor if it wasn't absolutely necessary.

Tarren reached up with the hand of his uninjured arm to undo the buttons, but Julia quickly moved in, pushing his hand aside, and took over releasing the small black buttons down the front of his shirt.

"One of them had a baseball bat and it connected with my right shoulder," he said. "If Raz hadn't alerted and I hadn't reacted, my head would have taken the blow."

A visible shiver ran through Julia as she slowly pushed his shirt from his shoulder. He appreciated she was careful not to jostle him as she helped to release his arm from the material.

She sucked in a sharp breath. He could only imagine the colors already forming in his skin. "Can you move your shoulder?"

Slowly, he lifted his arm a few inches but all of the tissues around his shoulder girdle protested. "I don't think anything is broken."

"You need to get it x-rayed," Jeremy said. "It's nasty. You could have a hairline fracture."

Blowing out a frustrated breath, Tarren nodded his agreement. "You're the boss." He gritted his teeth as Julia helped him put the shirt back on.

When she went to button the front, he stopped her with his good hand. "Leave it. They'll just need to undo it when we get there."

She nodded. He pushed himself to his feet and she quickly tucked herself under his good arm, wrapping her arm around his waist. He wanted to tell her his legs were just fine. But who was he to deny her the opportunity to help him, especially when she felt so good pressed against his side? The smell of the shampoo she used teased his nostrils and soothed some of the pain.

They piled into Jeremy's police vehicle. Tarren

sat up front while Julia and Raz sat in the back compartment.

Before they left the property, Jeremy talked to the officers who'd responded to the call for backup, giving them instructions to watch the property and for others to canvass the neighborhood to see if anyone had doorbell cameras that might have video of the perpetrators.

"Tomorrow, I need to get motion sensors, floodlights and an alarm system," Tarren said.

From the back of the vehicle, Julia asked, "Who knows I was staying at your house?"

"A small handful of people," Jeremy said, his voice reverberating with anger. "I will be investigating internally to find the spy."

They all fell silent as the ramifications of what he just said slid into place.

They had a cartel mole within their ranks.

EIGHT

The early morning sunlight streaming through all the windows stung Julia's eyes as she made her way to the kitchen, but the smell of coffee and bacon had drawn her from her room. Not that she'd slept much. Nightmare scenarios played in her head like a silent film. Over and over.

The taunting images of Tarren hurt, or worse, created waves of anxiety that only subsided when she turned on the light and spent time reading her Bible.

Tarren stood at the stove flipping fried eggs using his left hand. His injured right arm was in a sling. Thankfully, there'd been no fractures, only soft tissue damage that would heal with time and exercise. But the doctor had wanted him to use a support for a day or two.

"What are you doing?" She rushed to take the spatula from him. "The doctor said you were to rest and take it easy."

Giving her a lopsided grin, Tarren stepped back. "Cooking is not strenuous."

She moved the eggs out of the pan and onto plates. "Says you." She sniffed the air. "Where's the bacon?"

"Oven." Tarren moved to the refrigerator to grab a carton of orange juice.

"Tarren, go sit down. I've got this," she admonished.

Pressing his lips together to clearly keep from laughing, Jeremy said, "Sis, he's a grown man who is capable of taking care of himself."

She made a face at him. "That explains why Tarren's cooking but it doesn't explain why you're not helping."

Jeremy frowned and moved to take the orange juice carton from her. "He was already cooking when I got out of the shower."

Noticing the dark circles under his eyes, she relented. He'd stayed the night again as extra protection. Looks as if he hadn't found much rest, either.

Raz padded into the kitchen. The bandage had been removed from his shoulder.

"How's his wound?" she asked Tarren.

"Looks good. I talked to the vet this morning," Tarren replied. "He said as long as it's not bleeding, to remove the dressing and let it breathe."

She was glad that last night's incident hadn't reinjured Raz.

To Jeremy, she said, "Did you discover how the cartel knows I'm here?"

He shook his head. "Not yet. I've initiated an internal investigation to see if anyone in the department has ties to Rio Diablo."

"We'll figure it out," Tarren said. "For all we know, one of the neighbors could have mentioned to someone else that you and I are friends, and they took a chance to see if Julia was here."

She hated thinking that no matter where she went or what she did, there would be eyes on her. And people talked. Sometimes without realizing they were revealing harmful information.

"Yeah, well, we'll see," Jeremy said.

"Come on, boy," Tarren said as he moved out of the kitchen toward the garage. "Let's get you breakfast."

Julia hurried to follow him, but her brother's hand on her arm stopped her.

"Let him be," Jeremy said. "You can't baby him."

"I'm not," she protested. "I just don't want him to hurt himself."

"He won't," her brother said in a firm tone. "As soon as breakfast is over, you're coming with me to the station."

She drew back. "Why?"

"Tarren's arranged for an alarm system to be installed as well as motion detectors and floodlights," Jeremy explained. "This place will be crawling with workers. I need you to be safe with me."

"But what about Tarren?"

Tarren came through the garage door into the kitchen. "Daniel will be sticking around."

She remembered the young officer. "But what if one of the workers is a cartel member?"

"Oh, don't worry," Tarren said. "We'll be vetting everyone who steps on the property. If there's even a hint of a cartel connection, we'll be having a conversation."

The security measures would bring a level of comfort. However, remorse ate at her because Tarren was having to do so much to protect her. "I can help you pay for everything."

"Not necessary. I'd been meaning to take care of this stuff," he told her.

Still, it wasn't right. How had doing the right thing caused so many problems? And when would this situation be resolved? The questions bounced around her head with no answers, leaving her with a frustrated knot in her belly.

That night after another delicious meal, Tarren, Jeremy and Julia sat at the dining room table.

The installation of the alarm system, floodlights and motion detectors went off without a hitch. No known cartel members were among the workers, but Tarren and Jeremy agreed they couldn't be complacent. Just because someone didn't have a police record didn't mean they weren't in some way connected to Rio Diablo.

If something did happen, they had names and contact info to follow up on. Not that Tarren anticipated any more trouble. His shoulder ached but the over-the-counter pain relievers were keeping the pain to a dull roar. Julia had been fussing over him every chance she had. He tried to remember if she'd been as nurturing as a kid and couldn't. He didn't mind her need to take care of him and Jeremy. It was nice and made him feel cared for in a way he'd rarely ever experienced.

To distract them all, he brought out a card game from their childhood. Though met with a bit of lackluster enthusiasm, the siblings agreed to play.

As the evening wore on, Julia grew more pensive and Tarren could see the days had taken a toll on her. He nudged Jeremy with his foot under the table and caught Jeremy's gaze. Slanting a glance at Julia, Tarren said, "I think it's time to wind down."

"Right." Jeremy nodded, clearly receiving the message. "I think I'll head to my place tonight. There'll be a patrol officer standing guard outside here."

Julia set her cards down but offered a droopy grin. "I know you're calling it quits because I'm winning."

Jeremy scoffed and opened his mouth to refute her, but Tarren jumped in to ward off a competitive quarrel between the siblings. "Not at all," he said. "We've had a dramatic few days. I'm beat. Exhausted. Worn out and in pain."

With raised eyebrows, Julia gave a soft laugh. "Tell us how you really feel."

Tarren couldn't help but grin back at her. Affection unfurled in his chest. He'd always enjoyed spending time with her and he still did.

Julia grew serious. "Is the pain awful? Is there anything I can do to help?"

He reached across the table with his left hand and took her hand. "Really. It's not that bad. But I do think we should call it a night."

Jeremy stood, his gaze bouncing between them. "We can pick this game up tomorrow."

"Just remember I'm winning," Julia quipped as she moved to stand.

Tarren jumped up and pulled the chair out for her with his good arm.

"Thank you," she said softly and padded down the hall to the spare bedroom.

Aware that Jeremy was watching him, Tarren turned and said, "You sure you don't want to bunk on the couch, again?"

A speculative gleam in Jeremy's eyes had Tarren's heart pounding. There was no way Jeremy could know Tarren struggled to keep his attraction to Julia at bay.

"Dude, the couch is comfortable, but I prefer my own bed," Jeremy finally said. "I stationed Daniel outside. He's young and eager. I trust he'll stay alert. And you have an alarm system now. Plus, you have Raz."

They both turned to look at Raz, who lay on his bed underneath the front window. His dark eyes watched them.

"True that. I have you on speed dial," Tarren said.

Jeremy grabbed his things and headed for the door. Before he left, he turned to say, "Just remember, she's my baby sister. I don't want her hurt. In any way."

Heat flushed through Tarren. Had Jeremy somehow guessed the emotions swirling around him and Julia?

Without waiting for a response, Jeremy left.

Raz rose from his bed and nudged Tarren. "I know, buddy. It's past our bedtime."

After taking Raz out back and making sure all the doors and windows were locked tight in the house and the alarm set, he and Raz headed down the hall, pausing briefly outside Julia's door. The light was on, and he could hear her talking to someone. He rapped lightly on the door.

A moment later it opened. She had changed into the sweats outfit he had given her. She held her phone to her ear. "Hold on," she said into the device and then pressed the mute button. She met his gaze with concern swirling in her gaze. "Is everything okay?"

"Yes. Who are you talking to?" he said.

Seeming relieved, she smiled. "Mom and Dad," she said. "They're enjoying their time at Aunt Freda's."

"I'm glad." He wasn't sure how much Julia or Jeremy had told their parents. The Hamiltons were good people, and he didn't want them hurt. "Good night."

"Night." She backed away from the door and shut it.

He stood for a moment longer listening to the soft murmur of Julia's voice before heading to his room. Hurting Julia was the last thing Tarren would ever do and that meant keeping her in the friend zone.

Over the next few days, Julia did everything she could to stay busy. First, she organized Tarren's linen closet, then the bathrooms. When she ventured into his bedroom, he rushed after her. She stood in front of the sympathy card she had given him three years ago when his mother had passed way.

A warm pleasure infused her to realize he'd not only kept the card but also had displayed it in a prominent place on his dresser.

On wobbling legs, she moved to sit on the edge of the bed. Why had he kept it? She couldn't remember what she'd written in it and was too embarrassed to look inside. She'd been so busy preparing for graduation and Bryce had consumed so much of her time then.

Rather than ask Tarren about the card, she sought a safer subject. "You said you'd share with me your newer works of art."

"I did." He moved to the door. "Let's go into the living room."

She smoothed a hand over his comforter. "I like your room. Very masculine but not depressing."

"A strange observation. I'll take that as a win?"

"Do." A nervous laugh escaped as she rose and pushed past him, heading back to the living room. She didn't want to tell him about Bryce and how minimal he'd lived, or how irritated he'd become when she'd tried to cozy up his apartment.

As much as it hurt when he'd broken up with her, she was now grateful to be out of the relationship. Raz scratched at the back door. Before Tarren could get there, Julia let him out. "It's a nice evening. Why don't we sit out on the deck?"

"I'll bring the box of photos."

She slipped out the door while he gathered his most recent box of work and joined her on the deck. He handed Raz a bone. The dog took the bounty and lay down in the grass to chew.

As they settled in a pair of Adirondack chairs, he opened the box and began passing the photos over as he explained what they were.

"That's of the Port Isabella lighthouse at sunset."

Impressed, she slanted him a glance. "This is lovely. Did you know the lighthouse is used as a wedding venue?"

"I've heard rumors," he said and quickly handed her another group of pictures. "These are from the Padre Island National Seashore."

The northern end of Padre Island was home to a state park where the beaches, sand dunes, marshes and small ponds were preserved and cared for by the state. The park rangers would call the turtle sanctuary when they needed help with a turtle in distress and during nesting season. Julia and others from the sanctuary would comb the sand and tend to the nests alongside the park rangers.

She oohed and aahed as she flipped through the images that were magazine quality. "Whoa," she said, pausing on a shot of a large American alligator. "Where'd this bad boy come from?"

"I was fortunate to take this guy's picture before he disappeared," Tarren said. "It was both exciting and terrifying to be that close to a very large creature that could eat me. I alerted the park rangers. They know about him but haven't been able to capture him."

"They aren't native to the island," she said. "These guys typically avoid salt water but can tolerate brackish water for short periods. But there are some freshwater areas in the park. Did the rangers say if he was alone or does he have friends?"

Tarren laughed. "I didn't get into the particulars with the park rangers. I'm just glad this alligator wasn't interested in me. The park rangers said they can move fast."

"They can be extremely fast. That's why it's important when one is spotted to make sure they aren't anywhere near the turtles nesting or hatchings. There are so many predators preying on the turtles." She handed back the photos. "You're really good. I mean, like, professional good."

He was a man full of surprises. And she liked that about him. She liked him and found keeping her attraction to him in check difficult. But she would. Crushing on her brother's best friend as a kid was one thing but letting herself fall for Tarren as an adult would wreak havoc on them all.

Julia's compliment warmed Tarren's heart. He couldn't deny how much her appreciation of his photography meant to him. He didn't often share his work with others.

"It's just a hobby." He handed her another group of pictures and watched her as she studied the images. He enjoyed the way the corners of her mouth lifted and her lips parted when she liked a photo. The way her eyes flared with pleasure. His gaze traced the straight line of her nose to the tip that slightly arched upward. The curve of her jaw and the way her hair teased the contour of her neck had his pulse thrumming.

He remembered the sweet, surprised expression on her face when she'd seen the card she'd sent him on his dresser. He'd had to clench his fist to keep from reaching for her then just as he had to resist doing so now.

That she'd be touched by such a simple thing as his keeping and displaying a greeting card made him contemplate other ways he might please her. Which had him drawing in a sharp breath.

He was a man, after all, and she was a beautiful, sensitive and capable woman who made him yearn for more than he could ask for or give.

Jeremy's warning played through his mind like a megaphone.

Just remember, she's my baby sister. I don't want her hurt. In any way.

"Some of these should be in a travel magazine or on a travel site," she said, drawing his attention away from his thoughts and back to a safer topic. "These ones of the arches are stunning."

"Those are outside of Moab, Utah. The Arches National Park," he told her. "I took a trip up there after my mom passed. I needed to clear my head."

She met his gaze, her eyes soft and tender. "Understandable."

His gaze dropped to her lips. It would be such an easy thing to lean toward her and kiss her. Uh-oh. Keeping her in the friend zone was proving difficult. He cleared his throat. "It's the lighting."

"What?" She sounded confused and slightly breathless.

Had she experienced the same tremor of attraction?

Focusing on the picture in her hand, he said, "I had an instructor once tell me that photography becomes art when you can see the layers of light."

"Sounds very existential," she said.

"Perhaps." He studied a photo as memories of that time surfaced. He'd been grieving his mother, but he'd also been battling the guilt of relief. He'd wandered through the park for hours, lost in the beauty of the landscape that seemed to ease his suffering. "There's a way the light reflects through a lens that's indiscernible with the naked eye. It took me a while to see the layers but once I did… It's amazing how different angles of light can change the composition of an image. Not sure if it's the light and dark, or tone, but the very essence of the subject can be illuminated in ways that humans can't perceive through sight alone."

The way she stared at him as if seeing him for the first time had his nerves jumping. The yearning to draw her closer was strong but he held himself still. It wouldn't do either of them any good to give in to temptation.

She blinked, breaking the connection. She

handed back the pictures. "When did you discover you liked photography?"

He put the lid on the box, sealing away the photos once again. If only he could seal away the answer to her question.

Watching Raz abandon his chew bone in favor of a toy and trot around the yard, Tarren thought about dodging her query as he'd normally do, but with Julia, he didn't want there to be any more secrets. He answered honestly. "My father. One of the last gifts he gave me before he abandoned us was that old Kodak sitting on my bookshelf."

She put a hand on his arm as if sensing that talking of his father was painful. "Are you in touch with your father?"

He scoffed. "No."

"Do you know where he is?"

"I did," he said, not liking the bitter tone in his voice. He wanted to be over the past. He didn't want the hurt to have any more power over him. "He occasionally would send me a postcard. I would hide them from my mother. But she found them. I think it's what set off her last drinking binge that put her into sepsis. He didn't show up for the funeral."

"That's rough and a lot to deal with."

The empathy in her voice made him uncomfortable. He wanted to get up and walk away. He didn't like when people expressed sympathy for something he had no control over.

The warmth of her hand seeped through his shirt. He stared at her hand, small yet strong. Nails trimmed but unpainted. No jewelry. He wondered about the guy she'd dated while in college. Jeremy hadn't thought much of the man but then again, would anyone be good enough for his little sister?

Would Tarren?

Where'd that thought come from? Best to not let those kinds of musings take root.

"You are a good man, Tarren," she said. "I hope you know that. Your father leaving you doesn't define you."

He met her gaze. There, in the depth, he glimpsed pain. Was she so empathetic that she was taking on his hurt? Or did she carry her own burden? "Define me, no. Define how I operate in the world, yes. Too much."

A sad smile touched her mouth and deepened the soulfulness of her eyes. "I get that. Painful circumstances leave a mark."

There was something behind her words, he just didn't know the story. He wanted to know. To be there for her to confide in and let him take some of her burden. He covered her hand on his arm and threaded their fingers together. Reminding himself they were relegated to the friend zone, he asked gently, "Speaking from experience?"

She tried to tug her hand away.

But he held on. "I like to think we're friends,

Julia. Friends who share with each other not only the good times but the bad."

Tension radiated off her but finally, she nodded. "I am speaking from experience. Certainly not as traumatic as what you went through. In fact, my little drama seems petty."

Protest rose in his chest. "If it hurt you, it's not petty."

She stared out at the backyard. Raz sniffed the ground, following a scent trail, most likely catching the residual odor of the intruders. The spring leaves were green and small buds promised flowers on the pear trees. But Tarren sensed Julia wasn't seeing his landscaping or Raz, but rather something in her own memories.

NINE

"I would hazard a guess that Jeremy told you I was dating someone through college." Julia's pretty eyes were clear and trusting but there was a hint of pain, or maybe grief, in the blue depths.

Despite the warm afternoon sun overhead bathing them on the back deck of Tarren's house, a chill slithered down his spine, and his heart rate ticked up. She was hurting. "Yes. But he said you broke up with him after graduation before moving back here."

"I didn't break up with him," she said, her voice grim. "He left me."

The news was unexpected. Why would anyone choose not to be in Julia's life? His lip curled in disgust, Tarren couldn't stop himself from saying, "Then he's an idiot."

Her gaze softened, smoothing out the rough edges of the pain he'd glimpsed. "You're sweet to say so. And correct." She heaved a sigh filled with what Tarren could only categorize as regret. "Of course, I didn't realize that until it was all over."

He tightened his hold on her hand, grateful she was sharing details of her life with him. "Sometimes it's hard to see the truth through our own lens."

One corner of her mouth lifted as if she liked that metaphor coming from a photographer. "True." She shook her head. "Bryce never really loved me, as he repeatedly told me when he informed me he was accepting a job in Seattle and didn't want to be tied down to a needy girlfriend."

Anger simmered low in his belly. "You're the furthest thing from needy, Julia."

"I'm not so sure," she said. "He did a number on my psyche. Only going to therapy helped me to see that his constant belittling and cajoling had been his way of controlling me to the point where I had lost myself."

Tarren hated that some lunkhead had played fast and loose with Julia's affections. Protectiveness surged and it had nothing to do with the physical threat of the cartel and everything to do with the emotional well-being of this amazing woman. "That's why you returned to South Padre Island?"

"Partly. That, and because I always wanted to work with the turtles and the sanctuary had an opening. But I had been ready to give up that dream to follow him anywhere." She gave a bitter laugh. "Come to find out, he only started dating me so that I would help him pass his classes."

Tarren squeezed her fingers, though what he really wanted to do was track down the loser and give him a dose of reality. "Sounds to me like you dodged a bullet."

She slanted him a glance rife with irony. "I seem to be doing that a lot lately."

The truth in her words made his gut clench. Did she feel safe here? He hoped and prayed so. "I'm not going to let anything happen to you."

"So you've said." She bumped him with her shoulder. "There are no guarantees in life."

The trill of her phone had her disengaging from him to fish the device from the pocket of her sweatpants.

"It's the sanctuary," she said, noting the caller ID on the phone's screen. "Hello? Wait a minute, slow down. Okay. Prepare a pool and text me the details." She ended the call and jumped to her feet. "There's been a report of a turtle in distress near the south jetty. I have to go. We have to rescue the turtle before it dies."

He stood and blocked her path to the door. "Somebody else can take care of the turtle."

"No! This is my job. This is what I do. You can't stop me."

Fire lit her whole expression, flushing her cheeks. He wanted to cheer because it was so much better than the moroseness of a few moments ago. He kept his tone modulated in an effort to diffuse her ire. "It could be a trap."

His logic seemed to give her pause. "You'll be with me. We can call Jeremy. He can meet us there. Nobody's going to try anything if I have the South Padre Island police in tow. You saw those guys who hightailed it out of the market. Once they realized police officers were on the scene, they bailed." She clutched his arm. "Please. I can't let an animal die because I'm too afraid to step outside of your house."

"Julia—"

A familiar determined resolve slid into place on her face. The same one she'd get when they were kids and he and Jeremy tried to ditch her. She wouldn't have it and would wear them down until they agreed she could tag along.

"I'm not a prisoner here. If you don't take me, I'll walk there if I have to."

He growled with frustration. She would do as she'd threatened. This was the Julia of his memory, the one who didn't take no for an answer, who would badger and push until those around her bent to her will. Unless he wanted to forcibly restrain her, he had to do what he could to keep her safe while allowing her to rescue a turtle in distress.

He pulled out his own phone. "I'll call Jeremy."

She practically beamed, then went on tiptoe to kiss him on the cheek. Her lips were soft against his bristled skin and sent a ripple of sensation cascading over him to settle near his heart.

"Thank you," she said. "You all should wear cold-weather rain gear."

He glanced at the sky, noting for the first time the dark clouds moving in. Weather in Texas could be unpredictable, even on the Gulf. "What about you?"

She headed for the door. "I had Jeremy bring me my gear when he brought things from my house."

Of course she did. Her turtles were her obsession and she'd planned to be ready in case she was needed.

He whistled for Raz. The dog came running. "Time to work, boy."

There was a heavy police presence and a gathering crowd of beachcombers by the time Julia and Tarren arrived at the southern tip of the island. A long stretch of stones, varying in size and shape, created a barrier to protect the beach from the tides and currents of the ocean.

When Tarren had said he'd call Jeremy, she'd expected her brother and maybe one or two other officers at most. But there were at least five South Padre Island officers, plus three men and one woman wearing navy jackets with *FBI* on the back. Her brother was wearing his rain gear, standing with his arms crossed over his chest and a fierce look on his face.

She grimaced. "Jeremy doesn't look happy."

"Did you expect him to be?"

A rhetorical question she chose to ignore.

Tarren brought the vehicle to a halt and undid his seat belt. "Listen, I need you to stay close."

"Aye, aye, Captain," she teased, though inside her stomach was twisting with worry, not only for her safety and those of the men and women here to protect her but also for the turtle.

Grabbing the bag of supplies she'd gathered from Tarren's garage, she quickly hopped out of the vehicle and made a beeline for her brother. "Did you find the turtle?"

"It's near the end of the jetty," he said. "The poor thing is tangled in fishing line and seems to be struggling."

Concern had her moving across the uneven stones of the jetty before she remembered Tarren's directive to stay close. She paused to wait for him as he grabbed the ice chest they would use to transport the turtle if they were unable to release it back to the ocean. He let Raz out of the vehicle and marched forward.

The way Tarren's eyebrows were drawn together said he was miffed, but thankfully he stayed silent as they made their way to the farthest tip of the long jetty. She really didn't want a lecture when she needed to focus on keeping her footing.

Ocean water splashed onto the rocks, making the way slippery. The briny scents of salt and decomposing seaweed filled her lungs.

Two officers seemed to be standing guard, keeping everyone else at bay. Several civilians stood off to the side watching. Julia guessed one of them must have called the sanctuary.

"It's a green sea turtle." She winced and squatted down.

Bright blue fishing lines wrapped around the hard shell, trapping its flippers. The poor creature's head was stuck in one of the holes of the net.

"How can you tell what kind of turtle it is?" one of the officers asked.

Glancing up, she said, "The scutes, or large scales, on the shell are unique to this species along with the one pair of elongated prefrontal scales between the eyes."

She set the bag she carried to the side, opened it and removed a set of pruning shears she'd found on Tarren's workbench.

"Okay, little fella, here we go," she cooed. She cut away at the tangled fishing wire wrapped around the medium-sized turtle with the pruning shears while keeping one hand firmly on his shell to keep the turtle from thrashing about and hurting himself more on the jagged rocks that he was wedged between.

Tarren crouched next to her. "How did he get up here?"

"A swell must have washed him onto the jetty and he got stuck. Green sea turtles aren't able to retract their limbs and head into their shells, which makes them vulnerable on land. It's a wonder a seagull hasn't made a feast of him."

"What can I do to help?"

"Place your hand over mine on his shell," she said.

He did as instructed, his big palm covering hers. The heat from his skin seeped into her cold hand. She eased her hand out from underneath his to work at removing the fishing line. "Hold him steady. The looser the fishing wire gets, the more he's going to thrash."

"I've got you, little buddy," Tarren murmured.

Julia's heart swelled with tenderness. She'd always known Tarren had a sensitive side. He'd always been kind and compassionate to her. But to see him be kind and compassionate to the sea turtle had her emotions roiling.

"This fishing line is a mess," she muttered, keeping her gaze on the turtle as she carefully cut the lines away. "Part of it is wrapped around these rocks, holding him in place. Once I free him from the rocks, we'll pick him up with whatever fishing line is left and put him in the cooler.

Then we need to get him back to the sanctuary pronto so I can remove the line around his neck. These shears are too thick and I risk cutting into the flesh."

"We can have someone else take the turtle to the sanctuary," Tarren said. "We're going back to the house."

She didn't want to waste time arguing with him. Instead, she remained quiet and focused on cutting the tethers holding the turtle onto the rocks.

The rev of an outboard motor drifted on the sea air. Probably a lookie-loo, as her mother would say, wanting to know what was happening.

A loud crack split the sea air seconds before something struck the rocks close to Julia. Bits of debris bit at her, catching her in the face. She let out a surprised yelp.

And another as Tarren wrapped himself around her, using his body as a shield. Her mind couldn't fathom what was happening until another barrage of gunfire broke out. Her heart leaped into her throat at the deafening noise.

Raz went crazy, barking and jumping.

She worried for the turtle.

Then the boat engine revved again and sped away. She became aware of shouting all around her. Tarren slowly released his hold on her.

She came up for air. Agents and law enforcement officers ran toward the beach. Off in the distance, the motorboat sliced through the water, going far out to sea and up the coastline.

Tarren eased his hold on her, allowing her to lift her head to look around.

"What just happened?"

"Two guys in a boat shot at you." He frowned. "You're bleeding." He dug into the pocket of his jacket and brought out a Kleenex. "This is clean." He dabbed at her face.

She batted away his hands. "Tarren. The turtle."

The poor animal thrashed against the rocks, battering his shell as he tried to flee but was still trapped. Who knew what was happening to his tender underbelly.

She quickly maneuvered to pick up the turtle, fishing line still stuck around his neck and flippers, and put it into the ice chest. "There's no time to waste. We need to get him to the sanctuary now or he'll die."

"Julia—" Tarren started in a frustrated tone that at any other time she would try to appease, but right now the turtle needed her more than she needed to address Tarren's agitation.

She grabbed the bag of supplies. "Let's go."

Tarren hefted the ice chest up into his arms. Julia led the way, glancing over her shoulder occasionally to make sure Tarren didn't slip. Razz ran ahead of them and darted back several times.

Jeremy raced over to the vehicle as Tarren

lifted the ice chest into the back. "The FBI are going to chase down the boat. Are you both okay?"

"Your sister—" Tarren began.

Julia interrupted him with, "We're fine. The turtle's not. We're going to the sanctuary."

"Excuse me?"

Ignoring her brother, Julia turned to Tarren. "You're either driving, or I am."

Tarren turned to Jeremy. The look of frustration that passed between the two men almost made Julia smile. She'd seen that silent exchange often enough over the years to know they'd agreed on a decision without a word.

"I'll have officers follow you," Jeremy said. "Then straight back to Tarren's."

She went to her brother to give him a quick hug of gratitude. "Of course."

His arms held her for a moment, then he said, "Go, save the turtle."

Tarren opened the passenger door for her.

Leaving her brother's side, she hurried to the vehicle and paused before climbing inside. She couldn't resist putting a hand over Tarren's heart. "Thank you."

The bemused expression on his handsome face made her smile as she settled in the seat with Raz in his compartment, his hot breath fanning her through the grated door.

Tarren drove quickly through the town with the

siren blaring. Julia acknowledged to herself that she was falling for Tarren, and at the moment, she had no idea how she was going to deal with it.

Tarren gripped and re-gripped the steering wheel while he maneuvered through the late evening traffic along the main boulevard dissecting South Padre Island from the Gulf of Mexico and the lagoon of Laguna Madre. Adrenaline still hummed through his veins.

Keeping an eye out for any signs of being followed by the cartel, he could make out the silhouette of the South Padre Island police cruiser behind them, which gave him a measure of comfort despite wanting to howl with frustration. Somehow the cartel had discovered Julia was at the jetty.

He didn't think the turtle had been set there purposely. It wasn't a predetermined trap. But someone had used the situation to their advantage and had taken pot shots at Julia.

And hurt her. The sight of the blood on her cheek had hit him square in the chest.

The shooter would pay.

He wanted to whisk Julia far away from the island and the cartel. But that wasn't feasible. He didn't like the idea of the turtle suffering. What choice did he have but to take Julia to the sanctuary? And then he was going to take her back to his house where they would be safe.

For how long?

He pulled into the parking space near the door of the sanctuary and hadn't even turned off the engine before Julia jumped out.

Understanding her impatience, he hurried to open the back hatch. When she reached for the ice chest, he nudged her aside. "I'll get this. You release Raz."

She nodded, grabbed the leash stored next to Raz's special compartment and attached it to his collar before releasing him. Then the two hurried to the front door and knocked on it. Tarren followed with the ice chest occupied by the turtle.

A moment later, her boss, Pattie, opened the door. She wore a rubber apron over jeans and a long-sleeve T-shirt. "Is that the turtle?"

"Yes. Is everything ready?"

Pattie nodded. "Just as you requested."

Turning to Tarren, Julia said, "Follow me."

Carrying the ice chest with the injured turtle, Tarren kept pace with Julia to a back space that resembled a hospital operating room.

Julia indicated the stainless steel table in the middle of the floor. "You can set the ice chest there."

After depositing the ice chest on the table, he stepped back. Julia and Pattie lifted the turtle out of the ice chest and placed him on a plastic sheet. The turtle barely moved. Tarren winced, sending up a prayer that Julia would be able to save the creature. Raz inched forward, sniffing the edge of the table near the turtle.

Tarren tugged him back. Using what he would describe as surgical instruments, Julia worked to carefully remove the fishing line from around the turtle, freeing its neck and flippers. Impressed by Julia's efficiency, Tarren admired her dedication and resolve to care for the turtle.

"We need to get him into some water," she said.

"A pool is ready for him," Pattie said.

Together they carried the turtle out of the exam room into another room that housed several aquariums and freestanding tanks of water, as well as several shallow pools. They set the turtle in a pool filled with a few inches of water.

Julia hustled to another room. Tarren and Raz turned to follow her but she returned a moment later with leaves of lettuce. She put the food into the water and stepped back.

"What happens now?" Tarren asked.

"We wait to see if he revives quickly or not," she said. "Turtles are resilient."

"And if he doesn't revive quickly?"

"Then we may have to drive him to the mainland. There's a facility in Corpus Christi that could better serve him than what we can do here," she said. "I just pray this little guy livens up soon. Green sea turtles are herbivores. The lettuce should be enticing." She hunkered down next to the pool. "He looks young."

"Are you sure it's a he?"

With a shrug and a smile, she said, "I don't. It could be a she. The gender of a turtle isn't visible until they reach maturity, which could be decades. If this one is a male, the tail will grow longer and extend beyond the shell."

"How long will it be before we know if he, or she, is okay? I'd like us to get back to the house sooner rather than later."

"It takes as long as it takes," she said.

There was no mistaking the steely gleam of determination in her eyes. She wasn't leaving the turtle until she knew it was on the mend.

Pattie joined them. "I can sit with…hmm. We should name it."

Julia was quick to say, "How about Jetty?"

Nodding, Pattie continued, "Jetty it is. I'll stay the night."

That sounded like a good plan to Tarren. He could see Julia wanted to argue.

"Julia," Tarren said, capturing her attention. "We're both wet and cold and need showers." Despite the rain gear covering his clothes, the material was damp and stuck to his skin. "Pattie will call you if there are any problems."

"Yes, I will call you the minute Jetty shows any distress," Pattie said. "We can reevaluate in the morning."

After a brief hesitation, Julia nodded. "There really isn't more we can do tonight. Only time will tell."

"Oh, before you go," Pattie said. "Bob Mortenson's office called to confirm for this weekend." Pattie glanced at Tarren, her eyes wide. "I wasn't sure how much to say. And I didn't want to cancel."

"I'd forgotten." The pensive expression on Julia's face had Tarren tensing.

"What is this?" he asked.

"The Mortenson Group, specifically Bob Mortenson, is our largest benefactor," Julia replied, her gaze troubled. "His son was in a class field trip to the sanctuary a few years ago. Bob Mortenson is a well-known and well-respected developer on the island and they're having a companywide celebration at the lighthouse with numerous VIP guests from all over the country. I'm scheduled to be there with our turtles. It's a huge opportunity to raise more funds for the sanctuary."

Tarren gritted his teeth and chose to keep his thoughts to himself because there was no doubt in his mind that telling Julia she wouldn't be doing an event on the weekend would become a battle of wills. He sent up a prayer asking God to please resolve this situation with the cartel so he didn't have to disappoint Julia.

TEN

At 3:00 a.m. the next morning, Julia's phone sitting on the dresser next to the bed went off. The sound jarred her awake. She jackknifed upward from a deep sleep. The turtle!

After assuring that Jetty, the turtle, was comfortable and safe at the sanctuary, Julia and Tarren returned to Tarren's house. Leaving the creature had been hard. Normally, she'd have been the one to stay the night, keeping watch.

She reached for the phone. The caller ID read BLOCKED. Why would Pattie call from a blocked number? The muscles of her shoulders tensed. "Hello?"

"There's nowhere you can hide, there's nowhere you can run," a deep, heavily Spanish-accented voice said.

Her heart hammered hard in her chest and the blood pulsed in her ears, making a swooshing sound that distorted the words. "What?"

"I will find you." The line disconnected.

Spit pooled in her mouth, and she choked, trying to swallow. Shaking, she held the phone away from her as if the man on the other end might reach through the line and throttle her.

Throwing back the covers, she jumped out of bed and ran across the hall to Tarren's room. She pounded on his door.

Seconds later the door swung open, and he stood there bare-chested, wearing only black drawstring pants and looking like he just stepped from the pages of a cologne ad. His hair was mussed, and he blinked at her, not fully awake yet. A large purple bruise covered his shoulder from where he'd been hit with the baseball bat.

In contrast, the oversized sweats she wore made her feel clownish. Self-consciousness had her squirming despite her upset over the phone call. She was still wearing his borrowed clothes even though Jeremy had brought her pajamas. She didn't even want to know what state her hair was in.

"Julia?"

Pushing aside her embarrassment, she shoved the phone at him. "A man called. Just now. How did the cartel get my number?"

Alertness swept over Tarren in a visible wave and he took the phone. "What did he say?"

"He said, *'There's nowhere you can run, there's nowhere you can hide. I will find you.'*"

Tarren placed his uninjured arm around her

shoulders, drawing her closer. "He can't get to you."

She melted into him for a moment, absorbing some of his strength. But the potent mix of fear and anger coursing through her veins heightened her awareness of his masculine scent, making her woozy. She couldn't think pressed against his side, cocooned by his warmth. The feel of his smooth skin and the flex of his muscles made her mouth go dry and her insides gooey.

No. She couldn't fall victim to the allure of closeness. Too much was at stake for her to allow emotions and attraction to veer her off course.

She pushed away from him to pace across the length of his room. "I can't live like this. The constant anxiety is playing havoc on my mind. I need to be outdoors. I'm not used to being so confined."

"I understand." Tarren moved to his bedside table and picked up his phone. A moment later, he was talking to someone, telling them her phone number, and asking them to trace the most recent incoming call.

Grateful that he *was* doing something, she paused, wrapping her arms around her middle. Nausea bubbled, but she held it down. Raz padded into the room, heading straight to Julia's side, and leaned against her. Needing his comfort, she squatted next to him, wrapping her arms carefully around his neck, mindful of the healing wound on the dog's shoulder.

Tarren hung up and turned to face them. "I know this is difficult. It won't be forever."

"Really?" Could he see the future? "How long will it be?"

When he remained mute, she rose and plunged ahead. "You don't know. So, what are my options? Remain sequestered here until Gomez or the cartel makes another mistake?"

She was sure Gomez hadn't intended anyone to see his face when he tried to abduct Amber. She slashed the air with her hand. "Should I enter witness protection? Leave my family, you and my life behind?"

She couldn't do it. Wouldn't do it. There may be some who thought starting over, living a new life with a new name and no history, might sound exciting, tempting even. But not her. She'd worked hard to get her life back. "How long would it be before the cartel found me? Then what? You and Jeremy wouldn't be there to protect me. You wouldn't even know where I was."

The pained expression on his face dug at her. She didn't want to hurt him. But they had to face the fact that Gomez and the cartel would find her no matter what she did or where she went. She had to live her life.

She squared her shoulders. Raz remained seated by her bare feet. "Two days. You and the

FBI have two days. Then I'm leaving this house. I will attend the Mortenson Group event as planned. I will be taking my turtles to the lighthouse, and I will fundraise for the sanctuary."

The grimace that crossed Tarren's face had her bracing for an argument.

"I know this is important to you."

The gentle, soothing tone he used had the opposite effect of what he no doubt intended. More anger bubbled up through the nausea and Julia clenched her fists. "Yes, it's important. But what's really important to me, Tarren, is my freedom. That man has robbed me of my peace of mind and my autonomy."

Just as Bryce had done until he'd decided she was no longer of use to him.

Never again would she be helpless, held captive to the whims of someone else. Gomez Iglesias thought he could intimidate and threaten her and that she'd cower. He wanted her afraid. He'd succeeded. She was afraid. But she wasn't going to let the fear win. She wasn't going to let Gomez win. She had God on her side, along with Tarren and Jeremy.

His gaze darkened. "If you would prefer to be somewhere else, with someone else, I can make arrangements."

Oh no. Distressed that he thought she didn't appreciate him and all he was doing for her, she hurried across the room to place her hands on his chest. The heat of his skin beneath her palms traveled through her. His heart beat a steady staccato rhythm that matched her own. "It's not the place, or the company, that I object to. I hope you know that. I love being with you, Tarren."

Her knees wobbled as what she'd just said reverberated through her brain. She did love being here with Tarren. Getting to know him, spending time uninterrupted, with the outside world kept at bay. But this couldn't last. The forced proximity along with the danger lurking around every corner heightened her emotions and her attraction to Tarren.

She'd lost herself once before. She needed to stand on her own two feet. Her future was on the line. "I need to be my own person and be free of this nightmare, but that can't happen until Gomez Iglesias is captured and put in jail."

"But the bounty will still be in play."

His softly spoken words sent a shiver through her system. His hands wrapped around her, drawing her close to him. She put her cheek against his heart. Within his embrace, she was safe and secure. Cherished. The way she cherished him.

The last thought slammed into her, making her breath catch. She was letting whatever was happening between her and Tarren mess with her mind.

She extracted herself and backed up. "Then so be it. You have two days."

Before she could change her mind and step back into his arms, and give in to the longing to kiss him, she fled the room.

Hours later, after showering and dressing in jeans and a long-sleeved shirt, Tarren left his room and found Julia and Raz in the backyard playing ball. The morning sky was gray with clouds rolling in from the Gulf and the air chilly with the scent of the salty brine of the ocean on the breeze.

Julia had also showered and changed into soft purple velour pants and a cream-colored top that hugged her curves. Her hair was loose about her shoulders.

Her earlier diatribe had gutted him. He understood her frustration and her fear. The cartel seemingly had people everywhere. But they needed to find a way to neutralize the threat to her life.

The mention of witness protection had sent his heart plummeting. No way could he let her disappear into the system.

Stepping out onto the back deck, Tarren watched the pair, marveling how right it felt to have Julia in their lives. Of course it felt right. She'd always belonged in Tarren's life. She was family.

But she wasn't just his best friend's little sister

anymore. She'd become important to him in her own right. As a friend, yes.

And so much more. And that scared him. What if something happened to her? What if he gave in to his growing feelings and she left him? Would he spiral like his mother after his dad left?

He didn't know and he was afraid to find out.

"I'm going to make breakfast," he called out, not necessarily because he was hungry, but because he needed something to do. He wasn't used to this much downtime. Neither was Raz, but the dog seemed to be enjoying the respite from their normal activities. "Any requests?"

Julia paused with her arm in the air, about to toss the ball. "French toast?"

Tarren nodded and went back inside. His phone rang just as he was pulling out the ingredients for breakfast. He glanced at the caller ID and picked up on the second ring. "Jeremy?"

"Hey. The FBI's tech guy, William, couldn't get a trace on that call," Jeremy said, his voice rife with irritation. "It was a burner phone and is now off."

"Should I remove the SIM card from Julia's phone and destroy it?"

"No," Jeremy told him. "William has rerouted Julia's incoming calls to him so that if the guy calls back we will be alerted immediately. Then, hopefully, we can catch a break and get a location before he turns the phone back off."

"She's getting restless," Tarren said, though *restless* seemed mild for how emphatic she was that they had two days to resolve the situation before she resumed her life.

"Keep her busy," Jeremy said. "She's obsessed with dominoes. You know, the game with the trains."

He did know. As kids, they'd spent hours playing at the Hamiltons' home. He'd been so taken with the game he'd bought a set, hoping his mother would play with him, but she never did. The set was still in the hall closet. "I don't think that is going to work for long. She's given us two days. She has some obligation on Saturday. I don't know that we can stop her from going, short of sticking her in a jail cell."

Jeremy scoffed. "That's not a bad idea."

Taking a breath to calm the rising annoyance, Tarren exhaled and said, "We are not doing that."

"Kidding," Jeremy stated. "Tell me about this obligation."

Tarren explained. When he finished, he said, "You can get more details from your sister."

"Let me look into this and discuss it with our FBI partners. We might be able to use it to our advantage," Jeremy said.

Tarren's gut twisted and the hairs on the back of his neck rose. "We will not use her as bait."

"I appreciate how well you are guarding my

sister," Jeremy said, his voice hard. "But I'll be the one making the decisions."

Tarren rolled his eyes. "You may be my boss. And you may call the shots. But you've entrusted her protection to me. So whatever scheme you come up with, I want to be consulted. If I deem it's not safe for Julia, then it's not going to happen."

There was a pregnant pause on the other end of the line. Tarren winced, wondering if he had just overplayed his hand. Not only had he spoken to his boss in a way that he would never do ordinarily, even if they were friends, but he was pretty sure he'd just revealed how much Julia meant to him.

Finally, Jeremy said, "I will take your concerns under advisement."

Jeremy hung up.

"Good for you," Julia said from behind Tarren. "Don't let my brother push you around."

Not wanting to make a big deal out of the fact she'd overheard him arguing with Jeremy, Tarren busied himself making the French toast. "Normally, Jeremy and I are in sync."

"But when it comes to me you never have been," she stated as she went to the refrigerator to grab the syrup. She began to hum softly.

Was that true? Something he would have to think about at another time. It was hard for him to concentrate on the task at hand with the scent of her shampoo wafting around him and her humming echoing in his ears.

Needing a distraction, he said, "You up for a game of train dominoes after breakfast?"

She eyed him for a moment. "I know what you're doing. And I appreciate you wanting to take my mind off the situation."

Was he that easy to read? "Okay. So, is that a yes?"

"Yes."

Her soft smile reached into his chest and squeezed his heart. It always had—from the moment he'd met her the first time he'd gone to the Hamiltons' with Jeremy. He'd been so nervous but then this whirling ray of sunshine named Julia had peppered him with questions and made him feel welcome and wanted.

A feeling he'd enjoyed, and still did, if he were honest with himself. But how wise was it for him to be playing games and bonding with her when any romantic feelings between them were doomed?

Later that afternoon, Julia found herself seated at a conference table wedged between Tarren on one side with Raz at their feet, and an FBI agent on her other side. The room was filled with law enforcement personnel from both the Federal Bureau of Investigation and the South Padre Island police force. Her brother, wearing his neatly pressed uniform, stood at the head of the table near a whiteboard where a drawing depicting the lighthouse and the surrounding area took up most of the space.

Also standing at the front of the room was Special Agent in Charge Clark Whitman. The older man wore a light gray suit, white shirt and red tie. His salted brown hair was short, and a pair of reading glasses stuck out of the breast pocket of his suit jacket. He had kind eyes and a demeanor that made Julia think he'd be a good boss.

Blood thrummed in her ears as she tried to pay attention to the discussion going on around her. It was so surreal. They were discussing her life and how to protect it. She hazarded a guess that important people, like the president or celebrities, must get used to this strategizing whenever they appeared in public.

Beside her, Tarren's tension came off him in palpable waves. He was not thrilled by this turn of events. He and Jeremy had argued about the situation last night and again this morning. She'd finally stepped in and told both men it was ultimately her decision. She was going to fulfill her agreement to be at the lighthouse representing the sanctuary. That had put an end to the discussion and now here they were making plans on how to keep her and the public safe.

"We will have undercover agents on the beach and mingling in the crowd with the Mortensen

Group employees and their families," Clark said. "It would be good if your officers stayed in uniform, giving a visible police presence."

Jeremy turned to the whiteboard to contemplate the drawing. Julia would have to compliment Officer Stacy Ridgefield when she met her again. Julia doubted very much her brother had drawn the lighthouse with such detail.

Jeremy placed several Xs in a large circle around the base of the lighthouse. "I will have uniformed officers stationed at these points." Jeremy turned his gaze to Julia. "How big of a space do you need for your portion of the event? And where would you be setting up?"

Aware of all the gazes trained on her, Julia willed the heat rising in her neck to abate and slowly rose. "May I?"

Jeremy held out the marker. "Please do."

Julia wove her way through the standing-room-only conference room to take the marker and then consider the drawing. She wanted to be in a space that was visible to most of the guests, yet nonintrusive to the Mortensen Group's festivities. She decided on the space to the left of the lighthouse entrance where a sizable lawn provided a barrier to the walkway that led around to the back of the lighthouse for beach access.

She put an X with a circle and her initials on the blank space. "Will that work?"

"For me, it will," Jeremy said. "Clark?"

Clark considered the board. "It's visible but if we need to get you out of there quickly it's not too far from the parking lot. We'll have snipers on the rooftops within a mile radius keeping watch."

She really hoped nothing would happen and they wouldn't have to spirit her away from the property. Tarren had already told her he would be sticking close, so she was tempted to put another X next to hers with Tarren's initials. Instead, she handed the marker back to her brother and made her way to her seat.

"All right, we have a plan," Jeremy said. "I want all uniforms to check in with me for your assignment."

Clark spoke up, "Agents, we will meet in the break room."

The meeting broke up and everyone filed out. Julia stayed in her place, not wanting to be trampled by the agents and officers squeezing through the one door.

After Jeremy left the room, but before Clark could leave, Julia hurried to talk to him. "Sir, I was wondering if you know Agent Kara Evans?"

Clark tilted his head and eyed her intensely. "I do."

There was no mistaking the wariness in his tone. Julia forged ahead anyway. "How is she?"

Instead of answering her question, Clark asked, "How do you know her?"

"We grew up here together," she said, refraining from mentioning that Kara and Jeremy were once a couple. She doubted her brother would want that information to become public knowledge outside of those who called the island home.

Tarren and Raz joined her. Tarren leaned close to say in a low whisper, "Julia, what are you doing?"

Clark's gaze bounced between them with speculation before he said, "I did not realize Kara grew up on South Padre Island. Were you close with her?"

Julia nodded. "At one time. When you see her, please tell her hello for me. Tell her we—we miss her."

Obviously intrigued by Julia's comment, Clark inclined his head. "Of course."

Tarren's hand on her elbow urged her out of the room. Through clenched teeth, he said, "Not cool, Julia."

"What?" She started walking toward the exit. "She was my friend, too. And yours, unless you've forgotten."

"I've not forgotten." Tarren sped up to stay with her while Raz moved ahead of them. "Don't poke the hornet's nest."

"I'm hardly poking anything," she told him. "Asking Agent Whitman to say hello to my friend isn't going to create problems for anyone."

Tarren grunted in response.

They left the building and climbed into Tarren's official truck. Raz settled in his special compartment.

"Are you sure you're okay with all of this?" Tarren asked as he drove them back to his house with their police escort right behind them.

"I have to be," she told him. She wanted her life back. And God willing she would have it back soon. "I pray nothing will happen, but if something does, then we have to catch whoever tries to hurt me and make them talk. Better yet, if Gomez Iglesias shows up, he'll be arrested."

"I'll be praying right along with you."

ELEVEN

"Put this on underneath your T-shirt and wear your jacket to hide the bulk." Tarren thrust a dark-colored ballistic vest at Julia when she came out of the bedroom dressed in her long-sleeved T-shirt with the sanctuary's logo. He liked how her cargo pants fit her long lean legs and the way the shirt showed off her figure. He still wished she'd reconsider and not attend the event today, but she was as stubborn as always.

She took hold of the body armor and stared at him. "This thing is heavy. And it will be way too big for me."

"It shouldn't be too big," he said. "I took it from the department's armory. It's what our female officers wear."

She made a face and headed back down the hall to her bedroom.

Tarren grabbed two mugs for coffee from a cupboard and set them on the counter before he went through a round of his physical therapy shoulder exercises. Though his right shoulder was still sore from taking the hit from the baseball bat several nights ago, he was functional. His grip was stronger after the putty exercises he had done through most of the night as he worried about what today would bring.

Julia returned and he smiled at the sour expression on her face as she moved to sit on one of the counter stools. "Ugh. How do people wear these?"

"You get used to it," he told her.

"How much weight?"

"You have one of the lighter ones, I'd say five pounds," he said.

She blew out a breath. "That doesn't sound like much. But I got winded just coming down the hall. At least I'll get some cardio out of being protected."

As he poured coffee into their mugs, he grinned. "Way to make lemonade out of lemons."

She wrinkled her nose. "I'd like a little lavender thrown in. As a de-stressor."

"Duly noted." He handed her a mug of coffee. "We have time for some toast. Though I understand there will be food at the event."

She waved away his comment. "I'm too nervous to eat anything."

Distressed by her fear and obvious anxiety, Tarren set down his mug of coffee and hurried around the counter to gather her hands. "You don't have to attend the event. Everyone will understand not wanting to leave the island."

The lighthouse was located at the southern tip of mainland Texas in the town of Port Isabel and directly across from South Padre Island via the Queen Isabella Memorial Causeway spanning over Laguna Madre and the Gulf Intercoastal Waterway.

She squeezed his hands. Her pretty eyes locked on his. "You're sweet to offer me an out. But I'm committed. Both to the event and to doing what I can to help bring down Rio Diablo. Or at least the minions here on the island. And if crossing the channel to the mainland will draw them out, then I have to be brave enough."

"You're very courageous. Don't ever doubt it." Tarren had figured it would be a long shot that she would back out.

And there was nothing sweet about him wanting to keep her safe. His interest wasn't just professional. He couldn't deny how deep his feelings for Julia ran.

But there was no way he would jeopardize his relationship with her or Jeremy by revealing anything, so he released her hands and stepped back.

"Raz and I will not leave your side the whole time." He'd give his life to protect her.

After taking a healthy swig from her coffee, she slid off the counter stool, hiked a brown leather satchel-type purse over her shoulder and grabbed her jacket off the back of the dining room chair. "Then let's go."

Julia couldn't shake the eerie sensation of being watched.

Of course, she knew people were watching her. The FBI agents, South Padre Island police and the kids and parents stopping by to hear about the turtles.

Still unnerved, she straightened the stack of Safe Haven Turtle Sanctuary informational brochures on the table in front of her. The sight of happy people enjoying the Mortenson Group's event on the Port Isabel Lighthouse State Historic Site grounds did nothing to ease her anxiety.

The spring day had turned out to be calm and temperate, but dark clouds gathered in the distance. She was glad she'd worn her lightweight, rain-resistant jacket rather than a thicker one. The crashing of the ocean rolling up the sand and against the jetties underscored the pleasant noises of the party.

There were other vendors here, several specialty food carts and booths from shops from downtown. There was a carnival-like atmosphere to the event.

The historic lighthouse, gleaming white against the gray sky, sat on the top of a prominent bluff surrounded by a well-manicured lawn.

There were several museums on the property as well as a dolphin research center to provide many educational opportunities.

Standing beneath an awning near the lighthouse's entrance, in the exact spot she'd marked on the whiteboard drawing of the area when her brother had asked where she wanted to be situated, Julia forced a smile.

But mostly she was aware of Tarren's gaze from where he and Raz had positioned themselves a few feet to her left. Far enough away not to draw attention from Betsy, an Atlantic green sea turtle that had been found cold-stunned on the beach long before Julia had come to work for Safe Haven. The decision not to release Betsy back into the wild had been made based on genetic defects that had diminished her chances of survival.

However, Tarren and Raz were garnering their own crowd of partygoers wanting to hear about Raz, and asking to take pictures with the beautiful black German shepherd. Julia was glad to see Tarren take this opportunity to talk up the need to add another K9 pair to the island's police force.

Yet, there was something else causing the disturbing sensation prickling the nape of her neck.

Glancing around, she searched the crowd for the face of Gomez Iglesias. She didn't see him. But one of the cartel members could easily blend into the throng of people gathered. How would they know who was an enemy?

She held out a brochure to a mother and father with two school-age kids and went into her sales pitch on how funding for the rescue, rehabilitation and release of turtles was made possible only through donations. She was gratified when the parents made a generous donation. From the pocket of her coat, she handed each child a baby carrot to feed to Betsy.

Caring for the sea turtles, finding donors and educating the public had helped her move on after being dumped by Bryce. It helped that talking to people about the turtles came naturally. They were amazing creatures. She'd fallen in love with the work as a kid. In retrospect, she was grateful for the turn of events that led her back home to the island and the turtles. If she'd stayed with Bryce, what would she be doing now?

She sent up a quick prayer of praise to God for orchestrating her life. At the time when her relationship with Bryce had imploded, she'd hurt so badly. But now—if her life weren't in danger— she'd say she was happy. Or at least glad to be doing what she loved while surrounded by people she cared about.

As the family of four moved on, Tarren and Raz came over. She locked eyes with Tarren. Her heart pounded against her chest. A potent mix of attraction and affection zinged through her veins.

This man had become so important to her, not just as her brother's best friend or even her friend. Whom was she kidding? Tarren had captured her heart from the moment he'd entered her life.

She could still recall that afternoon when Jeremy brought Tarren over and, for the first time, she became aware of him as more than just her brother's best friend. A lanky, dark-haired teenager with brooding eyes, he'd smiled at her in a way no one else had ever done. He'd made her feel seen. And he'd been indulgent when she'd peppered him with questions and had even seemed to find her antics amusing whereas Jeremy had told her she was a pest that needed to be locked away.

Big brothers could be like that, she supposed. But Tarren hadn't been her brother; he'd been an amazing person whose attention she'd craved.

When Tarren had left the island for college and the police academy, Julia had told herself she needed to let go of that childhood crush.

But it was back in spades and there was nothing childish about it.

Unnerved by her reaction, she resisted the urge to smooth her hair or straighten the collar of her blue uniform shirt with the small sea turtle patch on the breast pocket. The bulky vest beneath her shirt itched but she refrained from adjusting it. The whole point of wearing the vest beneath her clothes was to not let anyone know she was protected by body armor. Instead, she zipped up the jacket to keep her hands busy.

Between the wind and her hair's natural wave, she no doubt had loose ends sticking out of her work braid. And her long-sleeve polo shirt had green stains on the sleeves from the feed she gave to Betsy.

Intentionally breaking eye contact with Tarren by turning away to straighten the stack of brochures, she said, "You and Raz are a hit."

"Not as much as you and Betsy. I'm impressed by you, Julia, once again," he said, his voice smooth and low.

An embarrassed pleasure washed over her. "It's the turtle. They are impressive creatures." Stepping aside, she tended to Betsy, giving her a leaf of kale to munch on.

"Julia."

The soft tenor of his voice shivered down her spine. She glanced up, their gazes meeting again. There was a warmth and caring in his eyes that had her catching her breath.

Did he feel the chemistry arcing between them?

She wanted to ask but was afraid to because what if he didn't? She didn't want to embarrass herself or let on that her feelings for Tarren were deepening to levels that had her heart racing and her mind jumping forward, wondering if there could be a future for them.

The crackle of the radio attached to Tarren's

shoulder broke the moment. Jeremy's voice sounded from the device. "Tarren."

Julia focused her attention on a group of children that now crowded around Betsy's tank.

Tarren and Raz moved a few feet away, but not so far that Julia couldn't hear as he thumbed the mic on the radio and spoke. "Here."

"We have a suspicious package at the top of the lighthouse," Jeremy said, his voice grim on the radio.

Panic flared in Julia's chest. She glanced around at all the people going in and out of the lighthouse, and those milling about on the surrounding grounds, smiling and laughing. Enjoying themselves. Unaware that at any moment life could change. Were they all in danger? What was the suspicious package? Did it have anything to do with the cartel?

"I can't leave your sister," Tarren said into the device.

"I need you and Raz to check it out," Jeremy said. "Two FBI agents will relieve you."

Two agents that Julia remembered from the briefing that morning hustled over to Tarren.

"I'm Agent Tom Kessler," one of the agents said. "This is Agent Ben Grant. You're needed inside, Officer McGregor."

There was indecision on Tarren's face. Julia knew he didn't want to leave her side. He'd promised he wouldn't. But there were lives in danger.

Not just hers. Raz needed to go and check out the suspicious package. She'd seen the two at work when they had checked her sanctuary vehicle for explosives. They were good at their job. If there was something dangerous in the package inside the lighthouse, Raz would alert.

Stepping away from her booth, she put a hand on Tarren's arm. "You need to go. Take Raz and do your job. I'll be fine here with these agents."

Tarren gave a sharp nod. "You have your phone?"

She gestured to her duffel bag stowed under the table holding Betsy's tank.

The intensity in his eyes was unnerving. "I want the phone on your person."

The stubborn jut of his chin told her he wasn't going to leave her until she did as he asked. She hurried to the table and reached into the duffel bag. Her fingers wrapped around the phone. She made a show of tucking the device into the inside pocket of her jacket and closed the pocket's zipper. Then she said, "Go. Hurry."

Tarren and Raz hustled away, disappearing inside the lighthouse. Anxiety camped out in her chest as she waited, along with every other law enforcement person there, to see if they needed to evacuate.

Tarren and Raz climbed the metal spiral staircase of the seventy-three-foot Port Isabel Lighthouse. The air was musty and stale. Wind coming off the Laguna Madre, the local intercoastal waterway, buffeted the structure, creating a swaying sensation that had his stomach roiling. Or maybe the nausea came from leaving Julia.

He hated not having her in his sight. But he had a job to do.

At the top of the lighthouse, inside the lantern room, placed flush to the custom-made pedestal mounted with the acrylic reproduction of the original light fixture, was indeed a brown paper-wrapped box. Jeremy and two other officers waited for them in the tight space.

"Has anyone touched it?" Tarren asked.

"No," Jeremy said. "As soon as it was discovered we've kept all civilians out."

Tarren hunched down next to Raz and pointed. "Search."

The dog immediately perked up, his nose twitching as he smelled the floor leading to the package, then he sat and looked back over his shoulder with a soft whine. His passive alert. The dog was trained to know that a bark could set off an explosion if the device was wired to trigger off sound.

Tarren motioned Raz back to his side. "We need to evacuate and get the bomb technicians here."

And he needed to get Julia to safety.

The two FBI agents standing guard over Julia seemed to be listening to a hidden earpiece. Their stoic expressions revealed nothing of what they were hearing.

Agent Kessler lifted the sleeve of his jacket to his mouth and said, "Understood. Moving witness to SUV now."

Sudden chaos seemed to break out as law enforcement began evacuating the lighthouse and surrounding area.

"We need everyone to vacate the grounds now!"

Julia wasn't sure who shouted the directive but it got people hustling toward the parking lot. Parents carried crying children. Couples huddled close as they scurried away from the lighthouse. Vender booths were abandoned.

Where was Tarren? What had he found?

"Miss Hamilton, we have to go," Agent Grant urged as he tugged on her elbow.

"I can't leave my turtle," Julia said and secured her purse on her shoulder. "One of you help me carry Betsy's tank to the SUV."

Agent Kessler moved to the tank. "I'll grab this end." To his partner, he said, "You bring the SUV to the walkway. And open the back hatch."

Agent Grant released his hold on Julia and raced away.

Julia kept her gaze on the entrance of the lighthouse, willing Tarren to emerge. But he didn't. Just a crowd of partygoers exiting. The panic in the air was palpable. Her heart rate tripled. Jeremy emerged, herding people from the area.

Where was Tarren?

The screech of tires brought her gaze to the parking lot where a black SUV came to a halt at the curb. Agent Grant jumped out and ran to the back of the vehicle.

"Let's go," Agent Kessler urged.

Grasping the other end of Betsy's tank, they lifted the turtle's glass container. The going was slow as they had to make a path through the departing crowd to the SUV. A breeze whipped through the air. The brochures she'd left on the table in the booth scattered on the grassy hill.

When they reached the vehicle, Agent Grant was gone.

After securing the turtle in the back compartment, Agent Kessler shut the hatch. "Let's get you inside."

He motioned for her to come around to the driver's side and he opened the back passenger door.

"Ben!" Kessler yelled.

She glanced past him to see Agent Grant unconscious on the seat.

There was a scuffle of feet as several men rushed up upon Julia and Agent Kessler. One man grabbed Julia's arm and shoved the hard business end of a gun against her side. She was thankful for the body armor Tarren had insisted she wear.

Though it would slow the bullet down, maybe

even stop it from penetrating her flesh, there would be damage done, especially at such close range.

The other man, a teen who couldn't be more than nineteen, pressed the end of a long stick that had two sharp points against Kessler's thigh. There was a buzzing sound and the agent collapsed. Two of the assailants, both in their late teens, quickly gathered Kessler and stuffed him into the back passenger area of the SUV on top of Agent Grant and slammed the door.

It all happened so fast.

Panic and shock vied for prominence in Julia's mind. Her heart raced. Sweat broke out on her brow. A knot formed in her gut. She struggled against the strong grip digging painfully into her arm and opened her mouth to scream.

"Do it and I'll kill you where you stand," the man growled into her ear.

Willing to take her chances, she let out a scream that was quickly silenced by a big hand clamping over her mouth.

The teen swung the metal rod in her direction. Sparks of electricity danced between the two spiky points at the tip. Would that give enough of a jolt to stop a heart? Terror shuddered through her. Were the agents dead?

One of the other teens yanked her purse from her and tossed it onto the grass, the contents spilling out. She prayed they didn't notice the absence of her cell phone, which was still zippered in the inside pocket of her jacket.

With her wedged between them, the two men hustled her away from the SUV to the back of the parking lot where a white sedan sat idling. The same sedan that had followed her and Tarren before.

Julia searched the area, desperately trying to gain the attention of someone, anyone, to seek help. But people were scrambling into their vehicles, intent on leaving. No one paid her or the men any attention. The two young men practically dragged her to the back of the vehicle where the pop of the trunk lid unlocking sent a fresh wave of panic crashing through her and set off tremors through her body.

"No! No, no, no!" She dug in her heels and jerked her body, trying to break free as they pushed her toward the open trunk.

The older man slapped her across the face so hard lights danced before her eyes. Then she was lifted off her feet and crammed into the back of the sedan. The trunk lid shut with a definitive click, plunging her into darkness. The space was tight, with little room to maneuver. The weight of the ballistic vest anchored her to the trunk floor. She screamed and banged against the lid of the trunk with her fists.

The vehicle shifted as the men climbed into the sedan and the car slowly rolled out of the parking lot. White-hot fear sent her into a frenzy. Her fists hurt and her throat burned from her efforts as the sedan picked up speed, taking her to an unknown fate.

TWELVE

Kicking himself for leaving Julia's side after he'd
promised not to, Tarren pounded his fist against
his thigh. Yes, he had done his job. He and Raz
had found a bomb. But at the cost of losing Julia.

By the time Tarren had made his way out of the
lighthouse and back to where Julia had been, she
was nowhere to be found. His heart had pounded,
and dread zinged through his limbs like an elec-
trical current.

Chaos reigned. Tarren turned over the scene
to the FBI, who were scrambling to get a bomb
squad to the lighthouse. Agents Kessler and Grant
had been discovered inside the FBI's SUV parked
at the curb. Both were alive and groggy. They had
suffered burns where they'd been attacked with
some sort of modified cattle prod.

A shudder worked over Tarren. Had the assailants used the device on Julia?

After ensuring that the turtle, Betsy, was safe
because the creature was important to Julia and
she would be frantic to know, Tarren set out

through the throng of leaving guests, asking if anyone had seen Julia. He used his phone to show her picture, one of several he'd snapped when she had been playing with Raz. Of those still in the area, no one recalled seeing her.

Jeremy ran to Tarren's side. There was no mistaking the panic on his face. He held Julia's purse. "She's not on the property. I found this on the grass. She's been taken. Her phone's not here."

Fighting back a wave of terror, Tarren brought up her number on his phone. Her phone was hopefully still inside her jacket pocket. "I'll call her. Maybe she can answer."

Jeremy put his hand over Tarren's, blocking him from hitting Send. "The FBI tech guy has control of her phone. Let's see if he can track her."

Thankful for Jeremy's clear thinking, Tarren led Raz to their vehicle. Jeremy jumped into the passenger seat and got on his phone, while Tarren secured Raz in his compartment.

Within moments, the FBI's tech expert had tracked Julia's phone. Whoever had the phone, and hopefully her, had crossed back over to South Padre Island and was now headed north to the Port Mansfield Channel, also known as the Mansfield Cut, a waterway that separated the north and south sides of the island. There was no way across the channel except through the water. On the other side of the channel, the jetties protected the beach and national park.

"What's the cartel's plan?" Tarren sped toward the bridge taking them back to South Padre Island. The answer to his question slammed into him. "They must be intending to put her on a boat."

If the cartel succeeded in taking her out to sea, he might never find her. Tarren would never have a chance to tell her how much she meant to him. There would be no chance for a future together.

Jeremy's phone beeped and he put the call on speaker. "Talk to me."

Special Agent in Charge Clark Whitman's voice filled the interior of the vehicle. "We have a situation."

"Tell me about it," Jeremy groused. "My sister is missing."

"Amber Lynn was abducted from her home this morning," Clark said.

Tarren's breath caught in his throat. After Julia had saved the young woman from being abducted, Amber still ended up taken. "What happened to her protection detail?"

"They were overwhelmed by masked men. Injured but alive," Clark replied. "The parents were tied up and left unharmed."

Beside him, Jeremy rubbed a weary hand over his face. "Any idea where they are taking her?"

"Gomez Iglesias has been spotted in Corpus Christi. We're headed there now," Clark said. "Unfortunately, two more young women have been reported missing. One from Houston and another from Dallas."

A stab of anger jabbed through Tarren.

Clark continued, "And after looking into the two open missing person cases you have here, I'm reclassifying them as abductions."

Jeremy's fist hammered the dashboard. "Let me know when you have Iglesias in custody," he said. "We're going after my sister."

Trapped in the stifling trunk of the sedan, Julia had very little space to maneuver. The body armor made it awkward, but she managed to retrieve her phone from the inside pocket of her jacket. The bag of carrots in her side pocket made for an uncomfortable lump on her side below the edge of the vest.

She shifted off the veggies. Though there was little relief to be had. There was barely any air flowing through the tight quarters and she was beginning to sweat profusely. She opened the phone and flipped off the sound to prevent any notifications from making noise.

Not sure she should risk making a call for fear of alerting her captors that she had the device, she sent Tarren and Jeremy a group text.

Her fingers flew over the buttons.

Help! Kidnapped. Trunk of white sedan. No idea where they're taking me. Four men. They have guns and some sort of Taser.

Within moments, an answering text lit up the screen.

Tarren responded.

We're tracking you. Keep your phone on and hidden. Don't worry, Julia. I'll find you. I'm with Jeremy.

Though there was a measure of relief they were tracking her, the knowledge didn't stop the fear knocking at her psyche. What if they didn't find her in time?

Time.

How much time did she have? What were these men's plans for her? Were they going to kill her? Torture her? Assault her?

Time.

She wasn't ready to die. She needed more time. Time to figure out what to do about her feelings for Tarren. Time to have a future. Time...

"Get a grip, Julia," she whispered.

Tarren promised he'd find her. And Jeremy would tear the world apart searching. Between the two most important men in her life, besides her father, her chances were high.

"Please, Lord, be with me. Be with Tarren and Jeremy. Lead them to me. And keep them safe."

Taking strength from her faith, she took calming breaths.

Using the flashlight function on the phone, she

swung the light around looking for something, anything, she could use as a weapon. But there was nothing. She figured she might be lying on top of a spare tire and possibly a tire iron. Unfortunately, there was no way for her to get into the compartment beneath her.

She remembered something Jeremy had once told her. If she was ever trapped in the trunk of a car, she was to push out the brake lights. If nothing else, it would give her some air. Twisting as best she could to use her heel, she kicked at the brake light. The plastic casing cracked but it held in place. A groan escaped from her. She thrashed about, the blows doing nothing to alleviate the frustration, anger and despair tangling through her veins.

The vehicle slowed, then the terrain became rougher, the sound familiar. Her breath stalled. They'd left the main road and were now on hard-packed sand. Why were they driving up the beach? Where were they taking her?

The car came to an abrupt halt and Julia was slammed against the back edge of the trunk. Wincing at the sudden jarring pain, she quickly stuffed her phone back into the pocket of her jacket and zipped it up, seconds before the lock mechanism disengaged and the trunk lid popped open.

Three men stared at her.

The same two young men and the older man

who'd pressed a gun against her ribs. He towered over the teens. The malice twisting his face had sharp talons of fear digging into her soul.

"Let's go," he said, his voice hard and scratchy.

None of them tried to hide their faces. Did that mean they were going to kill her?

She screamed and kicked as the teens reached for her.

Despite her resistance, rough hands grabbed her, pulling her out of the trunk. The two teens dragged her along the beach while the older man stalked ahead. A fourth man, whose face she hadn't seen, backed the sedan up and drove away.

Frantic to find help, she craned her neck, searching for someone to come to her aid. But the beach was empty.

She recognized the Mansfield Cut, the channel that divided the island. A small aluminum fishing boat was pulled onto the sand. She jerked and yanked against the hold the teens had on her but they were stronger. The older man spun and hit her across her right ear. Her head throbbed with pain. Her legs buckled.

The man picked her up and dumped her unceremoniously into the bottom of the small watercraft. She rolled to a seated position and gripped the edge. The teens pushed the boat into the water. Before she could jump out, the three men climbed in. One teen started the engine and within moments they were skipping over the waves across the channel.

She hung on until the vessel halted on the white sandy beach of the north side of Padre Island. She was dragged out of the boat to where two ATVs waited.

A dune ridge separated the beach from the prairie-like grasslands of the Padre Island National Seashore Park. Deep in the park were marshes and ponds where wildlife was preserved. Few trees dotted the landscape, mostly willows and live oaks providing some cover. If she could get away, she could hide in the park, staying low to make her way north to the ranger station.

Letting her body go limp to make it more difficult for them to transfer her to an ATV, she held her breath in anticipation of an opportunity to escape.

"You," the older guy barked, pointing to one teen. "Get that boat out of sight."

"Why me?" he whined.

The older man lifted the Taser device. "No arguing."

The teen lifted his hands and hurried back to the small boat. Seconds later, he took off into the mouth of the Laguna Madre lagoon and disappeared from sight.

"Hurry, the boss is waiting," the older man said as he grasped her by the arm and lifted her to her feet.

She could only guess the boss was Gomez Igle-sias, who definitely was more than just a foot soldier.

The man forced her onto the back of an ATV with the teen driver.

"Don't do anything foolish," the man told her. He removed his black gun from the waistband of his pants. "I'm a good shot."

She forced herself not to react, despite the ter-ror racing along her nerve endings.

The teen started the ATV and hit the throt-tle. The two ATVs zipped up the beach side by side. She and the teen were closer to the dunes. She was surprised there wasn't anyone fishing on the shore or enjoying the mild day. Did the cartel have such a reach that they'd scared away any beachcombers?

The wind whipped around her, causing chunks of her hair to slap her face. Her eyes watered. The ocean was a blur. But she did note the large white yacht in the distance. No help to be had there.

Her only course of action was to escape into the park. She hoped the body armor would help protect her.

Bracing herself for impact, she jumped off the ATV, hitting the sand with a hard thump. She tucked and rolled, which was awkward with the bulk of the ballistics vest, and the gritty sand worked to slow her trajectory.

The two ATVs stopped in a spray of sand.

Not pausing to assess the damage to the various places on her body that stung from scraping through the sand, Julia scrambled to her feet. She climbed the dune, her feet slipping in the loose sand. She cleared the rise and ran as fast as her legs would take her into the Padre Island National Seashore Park.

Gunfire erupted. The sand around her flew into the air. She yelped and ducked, but she kept moving in a low crouch through the tall grass and marshy ground that sucked at her shoes.

"Oh God, please, be with me," she whispered the prayer.

Where were Tarren and Jeremy?

Tarren brought the vehicle to a halt. They had driven as far as they could. Water lapped at the sand. The area was clear of people and boats. Unusual for a Saturday.

The sedan that Julia had been kidnapped in was gone. Only tire marks remained.

Jeremy held up his phone, showing the dot where Julia was located. "She's in the middle of the park and on the move."

"We have to get to her before they kill her," Tarren said. "It'll take us forever to drive all the way around."

There was only one way off South Padre Island and that was back through Port Isabel and up Highway 77 to Corpus Christi. From there they could access the Padre Island National Seashore Park.

Jeremy dialed the phone. "The FBI has a helicopter."

"We can't wait that long," Tarren said. "Raz and I'll swim across. We'll keep in touch via phone. I'm going to find her, Jeremy. I can't lose her."

With an understanding nod, Jeremy stated, "We can't lose her."

A personal watercraft zipped around the bend of the north island from the lagoon and headed through the channel toward the ocean. Tarren didn't waste time but raced to the water's edge and flagged the rider down.

A man in his late thirties veered to the shore and brought the craft to a halt in the shallows. Tarren charged into the water, uncaring that his uniform shoes and slacks were now soaked with the salt of the ocean.

"Whoa," the rider said. "Am I in trouble? I didn't know this area was off-limits. No one said a thing at the rental place."

Reaching the man, Tarren said, "I need you to take me to the other side."

"Oh, uh, sure." The man scooted forward on the seat. "Hop on."

Tarren sat behind the man and patted the seat between him and the driver.

Raz splashed into the water and jumped onto the seat. Tarren turned to Jeremy. "I'll find her." God willing, failure wasn't an option.

After tripping and doing a face-plant in the muck, Julia realized the best way to hide how visible she was in the bright blue jacket and navy blue cargo pants was to cover herself in the sludge. She rolled in the marshy mud to hide as much of her clothing and her hair as possible, then tucked herself flat against a long, rotting log that had somehow made its way over the dunes and onto the marshy edge of a large pond in the center of the Padre Island National Seashore Park.

Probably some campers had dragged the driftwood log from the ocean and abandoned the piece of wood. A mosquito buzzed her head. The brackish smells of the stagnant pond water and grassy vegetation teased her nose. She stifled the urge to sneeze. Something teased her ankle. Chancing a glance, she grimaced at seeing a millipede trying to crawl into the opening of her pant leg. She flicked it off her with a shudder.

She wasn't sure where her assailants were, but she didn't believe they'd give up. They'd risked too much to abduct her and couldn't let her go. She could identify them, just as she could identify Gomez Iglesias.

Now she had four men wanting her silenced.

Tarren and Jeremy had to be frantic. She could only hope their ability to track her included through the park, where cell service was unreliable at best. Many campers had become lost in the park, ending up far from where they intended to go.

The 204 square miles of undeveloped natural habitat was beautiful but could pose a threat to the inexperienced or unprepared. There was no drinking water or shelter available from the elements. Which also meant there were very few places for Julia to hide.

Finding the log was a divine gift. One she sent up a praise to God for. But how long would it be before she was discovered?

Though the temperature was mild, with slight humidity, as the sun went down, the air would cool.

Wind made the tall seagrass surrounding the pond dance.

A splash nearby sent her heart rate into overdrive. She tucked closer to the log, inhaling the odorous smells of torpid soil and decaying wood. Had the assailants found her?

Turning her head ever so slightly, she glanced behind her.

A large alligator, at least eight feet long, slithered into the water on his short legs. Its massive tail flopped, creating waves across the murky surface of the pond. The creature's prominent, beady eyes seemed to stare right at her. The cone-shaped snout lifted to the surface and opened, showing rows of jagged, sharp teeth.

She stifled a gasp.

Was this the same creature Tarren had photographed? How had the beast found its way to the island? Occasionally an alligator would wash ashore after heavy rainfall in Louisiana or Florida. Clearly, this one had made himself at home in the park.

Barely breathing, she prayed with all her might the creature would leave her alone. She didn't want to become the beast's dinner. Measured as producing the strongest bite in the animal kingdom, the strength in an alligator's jaw was enough to tear through a limb like a knife through soft butter.

Men's voices carried on the slight breeze that had kicked up.

The tension knotting Julia's muscles ratcheted up. Her heart beat so rapidly that she feared the organ would burst out of her chest at any moment.

"We should leave her," one of the teens said.

"Yeah," the other agreed. "The mosquitoes are eating me alive." The slap of a hand on skin echoed through the air.

"You idiots."

She closed her eyes in recognition of the voice. The cruel man.

"We have to find the woman. If she gets away, we're as good as dead."

A shudder worked over her flesh at the remembered cruelty in her most recent captor's gaze.

Maybe the alligator would scare them away. She prayed so.

Opening her eyes, she searched the pond for the animal. The beast blended in with the dark water. Was he getting closer? Would the alligator chomp down on her and save the men the trouble of killing her? A whimper nearly escaped.

The alligator let out a throaty roar that echoed across the water.

"What's that?"

It was one of the teens. They sounded so close. Julia was surprised they hadn't discovered her. Nerves stretched taut, she prepared herself. She wouldn't go down without a fight. Willing herself to be still, she held her breath. Yet, everything inside her was coiled, ready to strike.

"An alligator!" The other teen's voice rose with panic. "I'm outta here."

"That thing will be the least of your worries," the cruel man said. "We keep searching. She couldn't have gone far."

The sounds of the men moving away had Julia releasing a silent breath.

Unsure how long to wait, she dared to break her cover. She scooted around to the end of the log and found herself facing off with the alligator.

THIRTEEN

Heart in her throat, Julia froze with her feet sinking into the marshy soil. Afraid to even blink, she stared at the alligator, its long scaly body visible in the late afternoon sun.

The creature had left the cover of the pond while her attention had been on the men chasing her and now stood only fifty feet from her, hissing a warning. Not such a great distance for an American alligator.

Despite their cumbersome appearance, alligators were wicked fast. Their short yet powerful legs could dig into the earth and rapidly cover the ground between them and their prey in the blink of an eye. Before she would even have time to turn tail and run.

Swallowing the bile rising in her throat, she sent up a silent prayer for intervention. She had no way to defend herself from the beast.

Fear-induced sweat tickled her nape. Her limbs shook with the effort to remain still. If she attempted to flee, the monster would be on her in a second.

Another noise broke the silence.

Barking.

A familiar sound that had icicles forming in her veins. Breaking eye contact with the alligator, she whipped her head to the side as a streak of black raced toward them.

Raz.

Full-blown panic blossomed in her chest. She let out a scream, "No!"

Tarren appeared over a small dune and charged forward. A sharp whistle brought Raz up short, a mere ten feet from the alligator.

The aquatic beast snapped his attention away from Julia, its sharp teeth gleaming in the waning sun. The alligator's powerful jaw shot open and shut as if in anticipation of a meal. Its long, large tail swished as he turned his body toward this oncoming threat as Raz snarled, baring his teeth.

Julia couldn't let anything happen to Raz or Tarren.

She waved her arms, stomping her feet as best she could in the muck, and yelled, "Here, alligator, over here."

Tarren's heart stopped for a full second. The sight of Julia, looking more like a monster from the deep lagoon with mud covering her from the top of her head to where her shoes seemed part of the marshy ground, facing off with an alligator had sent ribbons of terror winding through him, squeezing his lungs.

When the alligator turned toward Raz, Tarren's heart thumped and began to beat again. Raz was in danger, but Tarren was confident the dog would stay out of the alligator's reach.

But now Julia was trying to regain the alligator's attention, hoping to turn it away from Raz. As much as he appreciated how much she cared for the dog, he really didn't like her putting herself in mortal danger.

Stopping twenty feet from the alligator, Tarren called to Raz. "Heel. Now."

Instead of turning around, Raz backed up, keeping his eyes on the alligator as he moved to Tarren's side. Raz's tail stood straight up, and his ears were back. He'd stopped barking, but a low, threatening growl vibrated from his throat.

Tarren unhooked the safety strap on his weapon and slowly withdrew it, aiming the barrel at the alligator's head.

"Don't shoot it," Julia said, concern lacing her words.

The alligator's head whipped around toward her, as if he'd forgotten she was there.

"Julia, back away. In case you haven't noticed, it wants to eat you," Tarren ground out. He took a side step with Raz mirroring his move. Tarren needed to get to Julia's side to protect her.

"Gomez Iglesias's men are still in the park," she said. "If you fire off a shot they'll hear."

"That's a risk I'm willing to take," Tarren told her between clenched teeth. Her kidnappers might have heard Raz's barking. They could appear at any moment, but the more immediate danger was the alligator. "Back up and get out of here. We'll find you again."

The alligator's attention shifted back to Raz and Tarren. The creature's powerful jaws snapped between throaty roars that raised the fine hairs on Tarren's nape. Tarren had thought the first time he'd encountered this beast was terrifying, but having Julia in the mix was so much worse.

Apparently, the alligator considered Tarren and Raz more of a threat than Julia, because the beast turned his whole body to face them and moved forward several feet on its short legs.

Tarren put his finger on the trigger. He didn't want to have to kill the beast. It wasn't the creature's fault they were intruding on his territory. But the thing was menacing. What if some hapless hiker had happened upon him... Tarren shuddered.

Julia threw something at the alligator, something small and orange, which hit its snout. The alligator whipped its long head around to stare at her.

"Come on, you silly beast." Julia's voice carried to Tarren. "You don't want to be killed. Come on."

She chucked more orange objects at him. Were those baby carrots?

"Julia, stop it," Tarren said. Why was she purposely trying to aggravate the creature? "I told you to go."

"You're not the boss of me," she shot back. "We all have to get out of here alive."

Clenching his jaw so hard he thought he might break a tooth at her stubborn refusal to do as he asked, Tarren took another side step. Razz stayed next to him. The alligator's snout dipped down, snuffing the ground. Then he was chomping on the orange carrots.

"That's it," Julia crooned. "There's more." She held up a plastic bag filled with baby carrots. Tarren recalled her giving them out to the children to feed to Betsy.

Taking a handful from the bag, she reared her fist back and then threw a pile of carrots past the alligator. They landed in the soft soil, some sinking and some falling into the vegetation.

The alligator whipped around, presenting its back to Julia, clearly intent on finding the bounty of baby carrots she'd tossed at it.

"Hurry, Tarren," Julia urged.

Grateful for her clever ploy, Tarren patted his thigh to indicate for Raz to follow and then he ran the distance to Julia. Cupping her elbow, he dragged her away from the alligator, through the marshy wetland and over another dune.

They reached the other side and continued to run through the marshy soil and seagrass. In the distance, the water of Laguna Madre sparkled in the late afternoon sun.

Finally, Julia dug in her heels and stopped at the base of another dune. Figuring they were far enough away from the alligator, Tarren let go of her and came to a halt. He bent to put his hands on his knees and took deep breaths.

Once he straightened, Julia launched herself into his arms. He held her close, mud and all, reveling in the feel of her alive. He never wanted to relive those moments when he'd been afraid he was going to witness her being eaten.

Her arms snaked up to entwine around his neck. She buried her fingers in his hair and pulled his face toward hers.

A hair's breadth from capturing her mouth, he said, "Julia, you're caked in mud. Even your lips. And as much as I want to kiss you right now, the priority is for us to get out of here."

A shiver raced through her. "Promise me?"

Promise her? Could he? He did want to kiss her. Had for so long. And he'd inadvertently let her know he wanted to kiss her. But he was sure her actions were driven by adrenaline and fear. Not from any sort of romantic feelings toward him.

And he couldn't take advantage.

She was his best friend's little sister. Not to mention Jeremy was his boss and had the power to fire him. Tarren didn't want to do anything to jeopardize the life he had on South Padre Island.

Not even for a moment of what he imagined would be pure bliss. But what would happen when they were safe?

"I promise." Tarren couldn't stand the thought of hurting Julia. Or denying her anything. "You're still wearing the body armor."

She stepped back. "I haven't had a chance to remove it. Thankfully, I have a T-shirt on under or the thing would be rubbing my skin raw from all the running and rolling."

He adjusted his own much heavier Kevlar vest beneath his uniform shirt. "I hear you."

She frowned. "Where's Jeremy?"

Tarren winced. He checked his waterproof watch. It had been over an hour since he'd left Jeremy stranded on the beach. Where was the helicopter he'd promised? Had something happened to Jeremy? Tarren tried his cell phone but there was no reception. Even his radio was only static.

"I'm getting so fired," Tarren confessed. "I left your brother on the beach at the Mansfield Cut. I stopped a personal watercraft and got a lift across. There was only room enough for Raz and me."

She patted his shoulder. "I doubt my brother will fire you. And if he tries, I'll put up a stink."

Tarren couldn't help but smile at her words. She, no doubt, would do as she threatened. The idea that she'd go to bat for him had his insides melting. He tugged at the collar of his uniform shirt, the material sticking to his skin from the humidity.

The sound of a motorboat echoed off the lagoon.

They hurried over the rise of the sand dune, hoping to find help.

Julia dropped to the ground, nearly lying flat, and pulled him down next to her. He motioned for Raz to join them. The dog lay on its belly.

"That's one of the men who kidnapped me," she said in a whisper. "He must be looking for his friends."

Tarren kept an eye on the man in the boat, who appeared to be cruising the shoreline. Looking for Julia? "How did you get away?"

She glanced at Tarren. Her blue eyes, surrounded by flakes of muck, were barely visible in the glow of the setting sun. "I jumped off of the ATV they'd stuck me on and just ran."

"Risky, but brave." For the hundredth or more time, he admired her pluck. She was a gutsy woman. A woman who deserved all the good things life had to offer. A life with a man who didn't have a past that haunted him.

"We can head north toward the ranger station or back toward the Mansfield Cut," he offered, needing to keep focused on the task of getting her to safety.

"I wish we knew where the men who kidnapped me are," she said. "One of them is cruel. He enjoyed hurting the FBI agent." She gripped his arm. "Did the agents live?"

"They were taken to the hospital," he assured her. "Last I heard, they'll survive their injuries."

"Good." Relief poured from her voice. "The thought of anyone else getting hurt is too much to bear." She patted his arm. "Let's head back the way we came."

After belly crawling down the dune and out of sight of the lagoon, they hurried along the ravine formed by the dunes with Raz leading the way. Veering south, they made their way back toward where the island was divided by the waterway.

They skirted another pond. Twilight descended, creating elongated shadows across the marshy grasslands. The nocturnal noises of the park's wildlife rose on the wind. Though he had a flashlight attached to his utility belt, he refrained from using it so as not to advertise their position.

A frog jumped at them. Julia gasped, bumping up against Tarren.

He snaked an arm around her waist and held her close. "I've got you. And I think there's only one alligator in the park."

"That you know of," she said. "I'm not afraid of the frog. It just startled me."

He didn't argue because he had no idea if more than one alligator was making a home in the wetlands.

The going became more treacherous. Finding the protective cover of another sand dune, he said, "Let's take a breather."

She settled down onto the sand. "You wouldn't happen to have a handkerchief or wet wipes on you, would you?"

He took a seat next to her and Raz settled on his other side. With only the ambient light of the moon shining behind wisps of clouds, he checked the pockets of his utility belt and found a pocket with two packaged of hand sanitizer wipes.

She accepted one and used it to wipe away the mud from her forehead, chin and cheeks. "That stings."

He took the wipe from her and stuffed it into his pocket. "It's not meant to be used on your face."

Letting out a sigh, she leaned against the sandy hill. "The mud itched. Plus, it kept you from kissing me."

The petulant tone brought back memories of times when she'd wanted to be included in his and Jeremy's escapades and been turned down. He regretted turning down a kiss. He swallowed the lump forming in his throat. He had promised her a kiss when this was over. And he would deliver on his promise.

He reached out and brushed back tendrils of hair that had escaped from her braid. The ends were caked in mud. "How did you get so completely caked in gunk?"

She blew out a noisy breath. "Well, the first time I did a face-plant into the muck, I tripped over my own feet when I startled a deer grazing in the grass. Then I realized the mud could conceal this bright blue jacket, so I rolled in it. Like a pig."

He couldn't stop the smile from forming. "No one in their right mind would ever compare you to a pig."

"Oh, yeah?" Her teasing tone caressed him. "Maybe a piglet?"

He snorted a laugh. "Never. You're strong and beautiful and capable," he said. "Your family will be very proud of you."

"What about you?"

The husky quality of her tone had his jaw dropping and heat creeping up his neck. He snapped his mouth closed, thankful she couldn't see his face in the darkness. "Me? Of course I'm proud of you. You have shown such remarkable resilience. Not many people would have the guts to bail off a moving vehicle and brave the unknown in the wildness."

She was quiet for a long moment. Had he embarrassed her with his praise?

The unmistakable howl of a coyote echoed

through the darkened night. Tarren estimated it be to a few miles away. At least he hoped so. The park was home to many different inhabitants, not just the alligator they'd tangled with earlier. Coyotes, deer, snakes and other critters, both in the water and out, roamed the island.

It was the two-legged variety that had Tarren on edge. Had Julia's attackers given up? Or were they still out there searching for her? They wouldn't find them in the dark. But come morning, Tarren would make sure to get Julia to safety.

"How do you *feel* about me, Tarren?"

Her softly asked question hit him between the eyes with unwavering accuracy.

It was on the tip of his tongue to tell her exactly about the emotions crowding his chest. To tell her he was falling deeply in love with her. Had been for days, if not forever. But giving voice to those words would only complicate their situation.

There had to be a wall between them. A professional one. And a personal one. There was too much at risk. She was coming off a bad breakup and only starting to find her way again. She was being hunted by dangerous men. She'd almost been eaten by an alligator. It was too easy to think she was grasping onto some romanticized fantasy that wouldn't last once they left the wetlands.

How could it? He had no idea if he could make a long-term commitment. His parents hadn't exactly set a great example. And he didn't know if he could survive if a relationship with Julia went bad. The unknowns were too precarious. Taking that kind of risk was beyond his ability.

Needing to keep things light and to prevent her from spiraling down a road he had no intention of traveling, he bumped his shoulder against hers. "You remember that time we broke into the amusement park after hours?"

She let out a wry laugh. "I do."

He hated to hear the twinge of disappointment in her voice. He couldn't give her what she wanted.

"It's amazing you and Jeremy ended up on the right side of the law," she said with a tinge humor.

A feat he'd often contributed to faith in God and the murder of Coach Evans, their mentor and baseball coach. "We were intending to start the roller coaster up and take a ride, when, lo and behold, who should appear over the top of the fence?" He bumped her shoulder again.

"Jeremy told Mom and Dad some cockamamie story about going to the store for ice cream," she said. "I wanted some. And you both tried to ditch me."

"Yeah, we did. Thought we had, too. But you followed us right over that fence," he said. "I'll never forget seeing you hanging from the top. Dangling by your fingers. I about lost my dinner right then and there." Just thinking about it now had his stomach knotting.

She scoffed. "It wasn't that big of a drop."

A shudder worked through him. "Big enough that you twisted your ankle."

"Yeah, there was that."

Her rueful tone had him smiling, then he sobered. "Seeing you hurt then and almost seeing you hurt today—" His throat closed as horrible images played across his mind. Her broken and bleeding. Torn to bits. Gone.

She bumped him with her shoulder. "You carried me to the hospital."

"Thankfully, Jeremy found a way out without us having to haul you back over the fence," he said. Though he'd have done whatever was necessary to get her out of that amusement park.

"And you would've taken care of me that night." She reached out in the dark, putting her hand against his cheek. "But I didn't get hurt today."

He couldn't help himself from turning into her palm and covering her hand with his own. He threaded their fingers together and brought her knuckles to his lips. He kissed the muddy skin and sputtered to rid himself of the vile taste of the muck.

Her soft giggle wrapped around him, making it seem as if they were the only people in the world. His heart raced and the need to hold her overwhelmed him. He released her hand and threaded his arm around her shoulders, drawing her close. "When this is over and the threat to your life has been neutralized, we can discuss—"

Next to him, a deep growl came from Raz.

Adrenaline jolting through his system, Tarren jumped to a crouch, still holding Julia against him.

Something, or someone, was out there.

FOURTEEN

Julia braced herself. Something out there in the dark, across the prairie of grass and murky waters, had Raz unsettled. His deep growl continued to vibrate in his throat. The sound echoed across the suddenly still night.

"What do you think it is?" she whispered to Tarren.

"Only one way to find out."

The beam from his flashlight lit up the area in front of them and revealed a brown-and-black snake, with a distinct pattern of scales. The creature nearly blended in with the sand and mud on the ground as it glided through the tall grass.

"A desert massasauga," she said, recognizing the reptile. "They're timid snakes and resemble the Western diamondback. Same coloring and venomous, part of the pit viper family, but with no rattle."

"Good to know. Thanks, Tour Guide Julia." Tarren tracked the snake with the beam of light until it slithered away and disappeared into the night.

Not taking offense, Julia petted Raz. "That could have been bad if not for this guy."

Tarren shut off the flashlight. "I don't think it'll be back."

"But there could be others." Just thinking about the multitude of insects, reptiles and mammals that inhabited the Padre Island National Seashore Park sent a shiver of dread down her spine. Her skin prickled with the remembered creepy-crawly sensation she experienced earlier when the millipede had tried to climb inside her pant leg.

She may study wildlife and be versed in all of the inhabitants' facts, but she didn't relish any of said inhabitants getting too close. Turtles she adored. But nothing else. Not even the jellyfish that washed up on the shores.

"Raz will alert us if anything else comes our way." Tarren's voice held a note of confidence.

"I have no doubt Raz will protect us. That's what you've trained him to do," she said. "Unfortunately, I don't have any antivenin on me. Do you?"

"No. I didn't grab any from the back of the SUV," he said. "I wasn't expecting to go exploring in the wilds of nature today and I didn't have time to gear up for the trek."

She scoffed out a laugh. "Understatement."

Another low growl emanated from Raz.

"What now?" She groused in a whisper.

Tarren turned on the flashlight again, allowing the beam to illuminate the ground around them, but nothing showed in the light. She held her breath as Tarren made a sweeping arc, farther afield until the beam of light exposed a coyote. His reflected beady eyes glowed, making the orbs appear white and scary.

"There might be a den of them." A lone coyote scouting areas for the pack to hunt.

Raz's growl grew more menacing and rose in volume.

Without a sound, the coyote turned and dashed away.

Tarren once again turned off the flashlight.

The sound of him unbuckling his weapon had her tensing. "What are you doing?"

"I have my sidearm ready," he said. "I don't think the coyote will be back. I think Raz is enough of a threat to keep the beast and any others at bay. But to be sure, I'll be ready."

Raz seemed to relax now that the danger had passed. She could make out the reflective lettering of his police K9 vest as the dog folded his legs beneath him and lay down on the sand at her and Tarren's feet. Their first line of defense. She was going to get Raz a new chew toy when they returned home.

She tried to get comfortable as she burrowed into the sand beneath her and at her back, but the bulky body armor made it impossible. "I have to get this thing off me."

Beside her, Tarren shifted as if he, too, were finding comfort difficult. "Thing?"

"The vest." She unzipped her jacket, the material stiff from the mud, and pushed it down her arms. Then she pulled her polo shirt over her head. A chill seeped into her exposed arms and neck. She undid the straps of the ballistics vest, the out-of-place noise of Velcro ripping apart split through the night and made her flinch. The T-shirt she wore underneath the vest was soaked with sweat. Cold invaded her body all the way to her bones. Her teeth chattered and she was helpless to stop it.

"Do you need help?"

She shoved the vest at him. "Hold this."

His hand brushed hers, warm and appealing, as he took the body armor from her.

She groped in the dark for her polo shirt, feeling along the collar for the tag at the back, and then slipped it over her head and stuffed her icy arms into the sleeves. The shirt provided little warmth. Then she slipped the jacket back on, zipping it up all the way to its highest point. "It's cold."

The ballistics vest was passed back to her. Tarren's arms came around her as he settled into the sand, pulling her against him. Pleased by the gesture, she sighed, relaxing into his embrace. Hold-

ing the body armor against her stomach, she laid
her head on his shoulder. "Thank you for coming. I don't know what I would've done if you
and Raz hadn't shown up."

"I told you I'd find you." His voice was an im-
possibly soft caress in the dark.

She snuggled closer, wishing they were somewhere else, somewhere safe. A place where she
could turn her face to his and he'd kiss her. She'd
longed for such a moment seemingly forever.
"You didn't have to come. Protecting me should
have been Jeremy's responsibility."

Tarren remained silent. She lifted her head,
trying to discern his expression in the ambient
light of the moon. But his face was all angles
and shadows.

"I made you a promise," he said softly. "I intend to keep it."

Which promise was he referring to?

The promise to keep her safe? Probably. The
promise to find her? He'd fulfilled that promise.

The promise to kiss her when this was over?

She certainly hoped so and would hold him to
it. Though if she were honest with herself, she
wanted more than kisses. The depths of her feelings wouldn't be denied. What she felt went beyond a crush. She'd fallen in love with Tarren and
she wanted a life, a future with this man who'd
risked his life to protect her.

She hoped and prayed he wanted the same.

* * *

The first rays of dawn broke over the horizon, glistening on the sandy dunes and creating sparks of light. Tarren usually loved to bask in the sunrise. But there was no time to enjoy God's beauty as He painted the world with hues of red, gold and orange.

"Julia." He nudged her. She still had her head on his shoulder.

Holding her through the night had been sweet torture because he'd wanted to sweep her off her feet and carry her to a place where they didn't have to worry about bad guys, snakes or other predators. A place where they could be alone to explore the burgeoning love growing between them. But that wasn't what she needed. He wasn't what she needed. Couldn't be.

He slipped his arm from around her, giving her another nudge. "Julia, we have to get moving."

The men after her wouldn't waste a moment of daylight searching for her. He needed to make sure they were off the north side of the island as soon as possible.

However, prodding Julia to move was an exercise in patience. She made small mewing sounds that shivered through him when she lifted her arms as if reaching for the sky. Sunlight revealed the dark circles beneath her eyes and the filth still coating her from bow to stern. But he'd never encountered anyone as beautiful as Julia. Tender affection filled his chest. This woman was amazing and bright and full of so much heart.

"Have to stretch a little bit." She stood and did some stretching exercises.

Catching himself staring, he forced his attention away and checked his phone for cell reception. He made a frustrated noise as he saw there were still no bars.

"We need to get to the beach," she said. "That's the best option for cell service."

His stomach grumbled, reminding him neither of them had eaten since the morning before. He'd spent many a stakeout without food. He could deal with hunger pains. But it was the lack of water that might do them both in.

Raz, alert and ready to go, panted, a clear sign the dog was thirsty.

"There are freshwater ponds closer to the ranger station," Julia said as if reading his thoughts.

"A distance we may not be able to cover," he said.

They went several yards before Tarren realized that Julia had left behind the body armor. He pulled up short. "Go get that, we need it. You may need it."

She made a face and retraced her steps, picking up the flat vest and sliding it over her forearm, then meeting his gaze with a challenge in her blue eyes.

He wasn't going to force her to wear it. At least, not yet.

In silence, they trudged through the muck across dunes built over time from the winds coming off the Gulf. They happened upon a family of white-tailed deer grazing on the grass. A mama, papa and two juveniles.

Tarren wished he had his camera. The sight of the deer was beautiful with the early morning sunlight highlighting the whites of their tails.

Leading Julia and Raz in an arc around the deer family, Tarren noted that papa and mama deer watched them, their bodies coiled and ready at any moment to spring into action. They wouldn't attack them, but they would run away. He didn't want to disturb them.

They drew closer to the Mansfield Cut when the sounds of humans carried on the breeze.

Ducking low, they moved in a crouch to a spot where they could view the beach where two dunes created a narrow V shape.

A boat full of men disembarked onto the beach.

"Spread out," one man barked.

Julia gripped Tarren's arm. "That's the cruel one."

Tugging her back, Tarren made a decision. "We need to head north toward the ranger station. We'll cut across to the beach a few miles away so I can call for help."

Julia nodded but there was no mistaking the fatigue on her pretty face. This was taking a toll.

"Put the vest on," he said, not willing to take any chances with her life.

When she started to unzip her jacket, he stopped her hands. Then he took the vest and helped her into it, sliding the body armor over her jacket. There was no reason to hide it now.

Keeping low as they moved inland along the Gulf side of the island and staying in the path of the dunes for cover, Tarren kept Julia tucked against him. They hustled at a good pace. Hopefully, they'd be putting a great distance between them and the men after Julia. Raz stayed just ahead of them, constantly looking back over his shoulder as if checking on them.

Even Raz sensed how precarious the situation was becoming.

Between hunger and dehydration, their bodies would give out before they made it to the ranger station. He needed to get to the beach. He prayed he found a signal to make a call.

Checking the time and distance on his dive watch, he estimated they were a good five miles ahead of their pursuers. It was time to break cover and head for the beach.

He slowed and veered Julia toward the dunes. They would need to climb over them to reach the beach. "You still have your phone?"

Julia unzipped the inside pocket of her jacket

and produced her phone. "Not much battery left, though."

"Then power it down. Conserve what's left of your battery in case we need it."

Leaving the safety of the dunes and reaching the sandy beach, he paused to scan both directions. The immediate vicinity was clear. But far north of their position, he could see a vehicle approaching. Friend or foe?

He needed to get this phone call done. He had two bars; hopefully the signal would be strong enough to connect a call.

"I'll try Jeremy first," he told her and put it on speaker.

Within seconds, Jeremy answered. There was a lot of noise in the background on Jeremy's end. "Where are you? We lost the ability to track Julia."

"I'm with Julia. Her phone was about to die so I had her power it off. We're somewhere around mile marker forty on the beach." Tarren kept an eye on the fast-approaching vehicle. "The Yarborough Pass must be open again." He referenced the place where the paved road of the state park ended, and the beach became accessible to four-wheel-drive vehicles. "Sorry for the delay. I didn't realize the FBI had taken their helicopter to Corpus Christi."

Noting the vehicle gaining ground, Tarren said, "Please tell me you're driving down the beach."

"No, I'm in a Coast Guard vessel but the FBI are sending their helicopter."

If the approaching vehicle wasn't the cavalry… a panicked worry churned in Tarren's gut. The people driving their way could be civilians out for a beach day. Or it could be more cartel members.

"We'll keep watch." Disconnecting, Tarren tucked the phone back into his pocket. Julia shielded her eyes against the now high morning sun and searched the sky.

Feeling exposed and vulnerable, Tarren tugged her back toward the dunes. Before they reached the sandy hills, the *whomp whomp* of rotor blades filled the air. His gaze swung to the south where a blue-and-white FBI helicopter trailed along the ocean, heading in their direction.

He and Julia both ran out onto the beach waving their arms. Raz barked and leaped in the air, no doubt excited by the noise and by his human's actions.

The helicopter slowed, hovering over the water and banking toward the beach.

Julia turned into Tarren's chest as sand, pebbles and crushed shells picked up by the rotor blades beat at them.

The hairs at the nape of his neck rose as Raz's barking became a ferocious sound, nearly matching the noise of the helicopter. The dog had spun away from the helicopter. Tarren glanced over his shoulder just as bullets bit into the sand around them. He tackled Julia, taking her to the sand and covering her body with his own. Dressed in full tactical gear, the men tracking them charged over the dunes and onto the beach.

Tarren urged Julia to her feet. "Run for all your worth for the helicopter."

Sending up a prayer for their safety as he flipped to his backside, he returned fire. One of the bad guys went down. But there were so many.

Julia gave him a baleful look but scrambled to her feet and ran.

The sound of bullets hitting metal shattered through Tarren. He glanced behind him to see smoke coming out of the helicopter as it rose in the air. Their hope of rescue from the air was dashed.

Bullets riddled the sand in front of Julia, stopping her in her tracks. She screamed and covered her head.

A spray of bullets continued to pepper the helicopter as it rose higher, banking away from the shore with black smoke pouring from its engine.

On the beach, the SUV roared to a stop. Two more men jumped out, filling the space between Tarren and Julia.

Within seconds, Tarren and Julia were surrounded. Raz barked and snarled, ready to attack. Fearing for his partner, Tarren gave the dog the command to settle. With apparent reluctance, Raz quieted but remained poised to protect as he'd been trained to do.

"Boat's on its way," one of the men from the vehicle said to someone behind Tarren.

Turning, Tarren's gaze scraped over the cluster of men, searching for the one in charge. His gaze collided with the man Julia had deemed the cruel one.

He was tall with dark, unruly hair and equally dark eyes that radiated malice. He gave a sharp nod. The tactical gear he wore was high-end.

"I'd just as soon kill you both and leave your bodies in a pond for that alligator," the cruel one said. "But the boss wants to deal with her himself."

Tarren understood he was as good as dead. He just didn't want Julia to see it happen. "Spare her the sight of my death."

The cruel one's mouth stretched in a semblance of a gruesome smile. "If you both cooperate, I can accommodate your request."

That the man didn't demand for Tarren to drop his weapon told Tarren how arrogant this cartel minion was. Keeping his weapon at his side and trying to stay as nonthreatening as possible, Tarren mentally prepared himself. He would not go down without a fight. The first one to go would be the cruel one.

Barely breathing, Julia stared at Tarren, willing him to be safe. They'd been so close to escaping the park and the cartel.

But they'd been outmanned and outgunned.

She hoped the helicopter made it to safety, but she didn't dare take her gaze from Tarren. Her brother was on his way. The knowledge was the only thing keeping her upright. But by then, it might be too late.

Her blood pressure dropped. The world tilted. Adrenaline and fear wreaked havoc on her system. She was crashing. She shook her head to clear away the dizziness. No, she needed to stay alert. She needed to help Tarren. She needed to help herself. But how? What could she do?

Despair crawled up her spine and settled at the edge of her mind like a snake poised to strike.

A motorboat skimmed over the surface of the ocean and beached on the sand near where they stood. Two more men came ashore.

The cruel one gestured to the boat. "All of you, escort our prize. Kill her if she tries anything. The boss will take her dead. He'd just prefer to do it himself."

The cruel one turned toward Tarren. "I'll deal with this one."

Julia's breath stalled in her lungs. There was no way out of this. She couldn't let Tarren die not knowing that she loved him. A whimper escaped her.

As she was dragged to the boat, she yelled, "Tarren, I love you."

She barely had the energy to climb aboard.

"Please," she pleaded with her captors. "Don't hurt him."

She met Tarren's gaze. The anguish in his eyes matched her own. Tears careened down her cheeks. She sobbed. The boat engine fired up and they backed out to sea. She twisted so she could keep her eye on Tarren as the boat headed out toward the middle of the ocean.

She sent up a prayer that she would see him again.

FIFTEEN

Tarren's heart sank, and a groan born of despair leached from him as he watched the boat taking Julia away speed farther and farther out into the Gulf of Mexico. Since she hadn't taken the SIM card out of her phone, Tarren prayed Jeremy would have the FBI tech guy turn her phone back on and track her. He had to trust that God would lead Jeremy to rescue Julia.

Because Tarren had failed to protect her.

Beside him, Raz whined.

"You'll never see her again." The man held an AK-47 to his chest, the business end pointed at Tarren's heart. A heart that was shattered.

I love you, Tarren.

Tears burned the back of his eyes. He couldn't believe what she'd said.

Concentrate! Tarren was no match for the weapon pointed at his chest. Even if he could get off one shot with his sidearm, the other man could mow him and Raz down in the blink of an eye. But Tarren couldn't just give up. While there was still breath in his body, he would fight. "You're just going to shoot me. Really? Where's the sport in that?"

Raz let out a menacing growl to echo Tarren's question.

"Maybe I'll just shoot your dog." The man shifted the barrel of the rifle and aimed at Raz's head.

Stepping in front of Raz, Tarren held up a hand. "No! He's only doing what he's been trained to do."

The man snorted.

Tarren didn't know if he could save Raz, but he had to try. Crouching next to Raz, he said, "Back."

The dog whimpered and seemingly shook his head. He didn't want to comply. But Raz was obedient.

The dog backed up a few feet. Tarren rose and motioned for Raz to continue his backward motion until the dog was almost to the dunes. If things went sideways, Tarren hoped the dog's sense of self-preservation would kick in and he'd retreat into the wilds of the park. But the dog was trained to protect his handler. If Raz witnessed Tarren go down, he'd break his stay and charge to help. Tarren had to make sure his partner was safe.

"Down," Tarren called to Raz.

Raz slowly folded to lie with his feet under

him and seemed to be lying on the sand, but the dog was ready to spring up into action at a moment's notice. Tarren prayed that his adversary didn't know enough about dogs to realize that Raz could cover the distance between them in a flash. "Stay."

Turning his attention back to the cartel member, Tarren needed the man to lay down his weapon.

Raising his hands, with his sidearm pointed in the air, Tarren said, "How about we both put down our weapons and deal with this like men."

The man seemed to consider. "You go first."

Tarren slowly set his sidearm on the sand at his feet and straightened. His heart jammed in his throat. He was taking a risk. The man could double-cross him and shoot him where he stood. But Tarren hoped that the man had some sense of machismo that would demand for him to beat his adversary in hand-to-hand combat.

Slowly, the man raised the strap of the gun over his head but kept the barrel aimed at Tarren. He bent to the ground, hesitating slightly before fully releasing the weapon. The man stood, stretching to his full height. He had to be at least two to three inches taller than Tarren's six feet. But height wasn't always an advantage. Not when it came to hand-to-hand combat.

They circled each other.

"What should I call you?" Tarren hoped to get

some information. If he won this battle, he would need to know whom he was arresting.

"You can call me Cinco."

"Is Gomez Iglesias the head of the Rio Diablo Cartel?" Tarren fished. "He's certainly not just a grunt like you."

"I'm no grunt!" Cinco's anger reverberated through his tone.

Undeterred, Tarren pressed. "Where's he taking the women he has abducted?"

"Someplace far from here where we can get top dollar for them," Cinco boasted.

Tarren held on to his anger. These lowlifes *were* selling women. Having it confirmed churned the bile in Tarren's empty stomach.

Cinco flashed his teeth and rushed at Tarren, obviously accustomed to using his size for intimidation, but Tarren easily ducked and spun away, out of reach.

Raz went nuts, barking and snarling. He was on his feet.

Not sparing his partner a glance, Tarren called out, "Stay!"

Secure that Raz would obey, Tarren continued to move in a circle with Cinco, each drawing closer and closer until they were within striking distance.

Cinco's arm shot out, his fist coming fast at Tarren's face.

Tarren deflected with his forearm, the connection jolting up into his sore shoulder. He gritted his teeth and used his other hand to jab a single blow into Cinco's throat.

Cinco stumbled backward, grabbing his windpipe.

Tarren took advantage of the moment and rushed forward, going low and driving his uninjured shoulder into Cinco's gut and taking him to the sand.

They grappled, each trying to wrestle the other into submission as they rolled across the beach. Cinco was strong but lanky and his movements were awkward.

Tarren excelled at this kind of down-and-dirty rumbling. Something he and Jeremy practiced often. Though with Jeremy, Tarren pulled his punches. Not today. Not with Cinco.

Releasing his anger, Tarren sent his elbow up sharply beneath Cinco's chin. Cinco's teeth snapped together.

Cinco roared. And slammed his fist into Tarren's jaw.

Pain exploded but he shook it off and landed a hard jab into Cinco's temple, knowing the man was seeing stars, then followed up with another cross jab to his jaw from the other direction.

It was lights out for Cinco.

Tarren didn't waste time. He flipped Cinco onto his stomach and yanked his arms behind his back. From his utility belt, Tarren removed a set of handcuffs and secured the suspect.

"Release," Tarren shouted.

Raz jumped to his feet and raced across the sand to stand on the suspect's back.

Letting out a breath, Tarren grabbed his phone and called Jeremy.

"We're coming via boat," Jeremy shouted into the phone. "Almost there."

Tarren could hear the motor of the boat.

"They took your sister." Tarren tightened his hold on the phone. "You have to have the tech turn the phone back on."

"Already done. She's in the middle of the ocean," Jeremy replied. "Be ready."

The line went dead.

Within moments, a thirty-three-foot U.S. Coast Guard boat zipped into view. The watercraft's engine sputtered out as the boat floated just off-shore.

Jeremy jumped out and charged through the water to Tarren's side. "What do they want with her?"

"This monster—" Tarren gestured to the un-conscious Cinco "—said the boss wanted to deal with her himself. Did they find Gomez Iglesias in Corpus Christi?"

"It was a bad lead," he said. "He's still at large."

Tarren wanted to howl with rage. "The boat

took off north. The best we can do is head in that direction and try to pick up her trial."

Jeremy indicated to a couple of Coast Guard officers who'd also come ashore to take Cinco into custody. Cinco came to as the officers dragged him through the water to the boat. Tarren had Raz jump into his arms and carried him as they followed Jeremy to the boat.

On board, Tarren released Raz, who set out sniffing the deck.

Tarren turned his attention to FBI Special Agent in Charge Clark Whitman. "Sir."

Clark, his expression grave, said, "We'll find her."

Tarren nodded and moved to stand at the bow of the boat where he had a clear view of the ocean and the island as it passed by.

He had to find her. And when he did, he'd tell her…what? That she was misguided in loving him. That he wasn't good at relationships. That he was afraid to risk his heart.

Would she think him a coward?

As much as he cared for her, no, loved her, he couldn't—they couldn't—

Far out to sea, a large white yacht bobbed on the water, drawing his attention. "What's happening out there?"

Clark handed Tarren a set of binoculars.

Using the binoculars, Tarren zoomed in on the luxury sea vessel. Sunlight gleamed off the white hull and bow. Men with guns were on the deck. His heart caught in his throat. The small motorboat that had spirited Julia away was tied to the yacht's side.

Julia was on that boat.

Julia drank greedily from the bottle of water that had been thrust at her once she'd been brought aboard the large luxury yacht. Soft blond oak floors and lush white couches provided a comfortable seating area. The yacht wouldn't be hard for the police to find. She could only pray they'd arrived in time. If not, at least there was a possibility her killers would be brought to justice. Armed men stood all around her.

Footsteps coming up from the bottom level of the yacht had her tensing.

A man Julia didn't recognize stepped into view. He was older with salt-and-pepper hair, brushed stylishly back from his high forehead. He wore an expensive white suit that made her think of some Bond villain. Was this the cartel boss?

Then Gomez Iglesias appeared. He was just as she remembered from when she'd kept him from kidnapping the teenager, Amber Lynn. Thankfully, Amber was safe in her hometown.

Gomez sneered as his gaze traveled over her and he made a face as if she were the disgusting one. She wanted to vomit. He reached out

and plucked at the body armor Velcro straps.
She batted his hands away. There was no point
in wearing the thing anymore. She was trapped
and vulnerable. She removed the vest and let it
drop at her feet.

"You have caused me so much trouble." Gomez
kicked the vest aside. "I don't like trouble."

"Sorry to inconvenience you." She held on
to her composure as best she could and met his
gaze.

He raised his hand to hit her but the older man
tsked, stalling Gomez's motion. With a curse,
Gomez dropped his hand and clenched his fists
at his side.

"Forgive my brother," the older man said. "I'd
like to say he was dropped on the head as a child
but—" He shrugged as he poured himself a drink
of amber liquid from a crystal decanter placed on
a long dark wooden counter and considered her
over the rim of the glass tumbler he now held.
"Alas, he was born this way."

Her gaze bounced between the two men. Different in many ways yet she could see the resemblance in the plane of their noses and the set
of their dark eyes. Gomez was lean and bearded
with an unkempt appearance while his brother—
older, she would guess—was the epitome of
suave. "Who are you?"

"Ricardo Suarez." He gestured with the glass
to Gomez. "What makes my baby brother my

best enforcer is he holds a grudge. You kept him from finishing a task and can identify him. We can't have that. And despite your efforts, he did manage to do what was asked of him. But you have made it so we have to take our operation out of Texas, so now you will pay." He gave a sharp laugh. "Just as your policeman will pay. Cinco will see to it."

Her heart hurt thinking that Tarren might be injured, or worse, dead, lying alone on that beach. What of Raz? Would the cruel man shoot the defenseless dog?

Grief clogged her throat. Her legs wobbled. She sank onto the couch.

Her elbow pressed against the phone still undiscovered in her pocket. She needed a moment to turn it on. Hoping to play on the man's humanity, she said, "I need to use the facilities."

Ricardo smiled. "Of course, I will allow it."

He nodded to one of his minions. The man to her left grabbed her by the biceps and hauled her to her feet.

Gomez blocked the path. "Why bother?"

Ricardo stalked to his brother and placed a hand on his shoulder, forcing him out of the way. "We are not barbarians."

Keeping a tight hold on her, her escort led her down the stairs.

Below deck was just as luxuriously appointed as above. Thick white carpet, plush white furniture and a large-screen television complemented the space. She was led down a short corridor. She screeched to a halt in the open doorway of a large bedroom. Her gaze landed on four young women, all gagged and bound, sitting on the floor against the wall and lined up like dominoes. She recognized Amber Lynn. Julia's heart sank. All this had been for nothing. Gomez had still managed to kidnap his quarry.

The guard nudged her toward the bathroom. She hurried inside and shut the door, locking it behind her. She turned on the water faucet to mask any noise she might make and took her phone out of her jacket pocket, quickly turning it on. She texted Jeremy.

On the yacht named Mistress of the Sea. Gomez is onboard. So is Amber Lynn. Tarren is still on beach. He needs help.

Immediately, an answering text followed.

Leave your phone on and hide it. We're coming.

It was too much to hope that Tarren was a part of that *we*. Tears burned her eyes and clogged her throat. Now was not the time for her to give in to the despair and grief threatening to pull her into a dark abyss.

She had to keep these men from killing her or

the other young women. She had to discover a way to give her brother time to find her.

The engines of the yacht roared to life. Spurred into action, she tucked the phone deep in the closet behind a stack of towels. The guard banged on the bathroom door. She exited and hurried down the hall to the open doorway.

Before her guard could grab hold of her again, she was across the room and on her knees in front of Amber. She gathered the girl close. "I'm so sorry. I'm so sorry."

Amber whimpered and spoke, but the words were garbled by the duct tape stretched over her mouth.

Julia was yanked roughly to her feet and dragged back up the staircase to the main level of the yacht.

Gomez Iglesias waited for her. He held a sharp silver knife with a curved tip in his hand. His brother, Ricardo, lounged on the couch, and a smile played on his lips. Ricardo may think Gomez was a psychopath, but she would hazard a guess they both were.

A scream gathered in her chest. The urge to run, hide, to fling herself off the boat was strong, but where would she go? They'd simply fish her out of the water. This was it, then. He was going to slit her throat.

Oh, Lord, make it quick and painless.

Gomez gestured with a flick of his free hand toward the railing and the ocean beyond.

She was dragged to the edge of the yacht. Salty water sprayed her in the face, mingling with the tears streaming down her cheeks. The large vessel skimmed through the water at a fast clip. All she could see was the flat line of the horizon as she stared out at the Gulf of Mexico.

Wind whipped her braided hair about her head. She turned to face Gomez. His dark bearded face twisted in a malicious grin.

She braced herself.

Please, Lord, please watch over my family. Please hold Tarren close.

Gomez strode forward and stopped right in front of her, his feet spread wide to counter the motion of the yacht through the waves. She could smell the alcohol on his breath as he leaned into her space to yell in her face. "No one can stop me. Certainly not some busybody turtle lady."

She closed her eyes. Tension tightened all her muscles. Despite the cold, damp air swirling around her, sweat broke out along her limbs. A sharp stinging sensation on her right biceps had her gasping. Her eyes flew open.

Gomez smiled and stepped back.

Blood gushed down her arm from a deep slice.

"That will let the sharks know there is something nice and tasty in the water." Gomez waved his hand like he was royalty on parade.

The guards on either side of Julia grabbed hold of her, lifted her off her feet and threw her into the ocean.

Tarren's breath caught as he stared through the binoculars and watched two men lift Julia up and over the railing of the yacht, sending her flying through the air and out of sight to crash into the ocean.

Had Gomez Iglesias killed her and then dumped her, leaving her for fish food?

Tarren dropped the binoculars, his stomach revolting. Despair and grief reached a hand into his chest and squeezed all of his insides. He dry-heaved over the side of the Coast Guard boat as it sped across the water to catch up to the yacht.

A hand on his back offered comfort. But there was none to be had.

Not even Raz's nudge brought relief. The dog must have sensed Tarren's anguish because he leaned against Tarren as if to hold him upright.

When his stomach was done spasming, he straightened and wiped the spittle from his mouth and turned to Jeremy. Tears swam in Tarren's eyes, making his best friend's face blurry. "I didn't protect her."

The hard jut of Jeremy's jaw softened. He shook his head. "This is not on you. You did your best. We can't give up hope. I refuse to give up."

"No, we can't." Gathering his composure, Tarren blinked back his grief and straightened his spine. He would not let the enemy win.

The yacht continued out to sea, leaving a wake of white foam.

Tarren grabbed the binoculars and searched the ocean surface.

There. Her body bobbed in the water.

Sick with dread, Tarren pointed. "There she is."

The boat pilot veered off course and headed for Julia.

"Hurry," Jeremy said. "We've got company."

Tarren's heart skipped and then flatlined for a full second as the dorsal fin of a shark appeared in the water fifty feet from Julia. Tarren unholstered his weapon and shot in the direction of the shark, hoping to scare the deadly fish away. The shark disappeared below the surface.

Raz barked, the sound drowned out by the boat's motor.

The boat slowed as it drew close to Julia. Tarren's heart stuttered. She was floating face down in the water, with blood pooling on the surface of the ocean around her.

Tarren undid his utility belt and Kevlar vest and dropped them to the deck. He toed off his shoes as well. To Jeremy, Tarren gestured to Raz. "Keep him in the boat."

Jeremy frowned. "What—?"

Before Jeremy could finish his words or the

boat even came to a halt, Tarren climbed over the railing and jumped into the water. His lungs spasmed at the shock of the cold ocean but he ignored the sensation and swam to Julia.

His front paws up on the edge of the boat railing, Raz barked his protest over being left behind. But Jeremy held him in place by his police vest.

When Tarren reached Julia, he turned her over and rescue-swam her to the edge of the boat. The Coast Guard officers flung out a lifesaver. Tarren hooked an arm around it and allowed the officers to pull Julia into the boat.

A smear of blood on the side of the fiberglass hull had Tarren scrambling into the vessel after her. "She's hurt."

Raz whined and licked at Julia's face.

Tarren's gaze went to the tender flesh of her throat, and he let out a relieved breath to see the skin intact.

The Coast Guard medic checked her pulse. "She's alive. Unconscious, but alive. We need to get her to a hospital."

"Where is the blood coming from?" Tarren nudged the medic aside to check her for injuries and discovered a nasty slice across her biceps and a lump on the back of her head where she'd probably hit the water hard, rendering her unconscious.

Clark had the pilot turn the boat around and head them back toward South Padre Island. Jeremy sat holding his sister's hand as the medic dressed the wound on her biceps.

When the medic was done, Tarren gathered her into his arms and cradled her close. His heart wept with need and guilt. And love. She was hurt because of him. He'd almost lost her.

His gaze went out to the ocean, to the yacht, fast disappearing on the horizon, and he vowed to God he would bring Gomez Iglesias to justice for Julia.

SIXTEEN

Julia woke feeling groggy and her mouth dry, like someone had stuffed cotton balls into her cheeks. She ached from head to toe. Her eyes blinked open and a world of white came into view. Was this heaven?

Then she realized, no, she was in the hospital, lying on a bed and hooked up to beeping machines that monitored her vitals. She glanced at her arm, which throbbed. A big white bandage concealed the knife slice into her flesh.

Her head ached as it all came rushing back to her. Being kidnapped from the lighthouse, being taken to the Padre Island National Seashore Park. Staring down the snout of an alligator. Tarren and Raz had found her, and then she'd spent the night leaning on Tarren's shoulder. Climbing the dunes and being shot at on the beach. Her stomach roiled as she recalled the boat ride to the yacht, leaving Tarren behind to die.

Tears gathered in her eyes and a sob escaped.

Warm gentle hands gathered hers. "Hey, now," her brother said. "You're safe. I've got you."

Her gaze snapped to his. She'd never been happier to see her big brother than she was at that moment. His skin had a pallor to it she'd never seen before on him. His eyes were weary and his face unshaven. His police chief uniform was rumpled and water stained.

Jeremy reached for the call button. "The doctor's going to want to know you're awake. You gave us quite a scare."

No wonder he appeared so haggard. "How long have I been here?"

He scrubbed a hand over his face. "You've been unconscious for thirty-six hours."

"Tarren? Raz?" Her voice came out as a croak.

"He's okay." He gave a firm nod. "They're okay."

"He didn't die." The relief was overwhelming. Tarren was still alive. And Raz was well. She couldn't wait to see Tarren and hear how he'd managed to survive. "Where is he?"

"Out hunting right now," Jeremy said.

His words swirled in her fuzzy mind. Hunting? She blinked to focus. "What?"

Jeremy smiled. "He's gone after Gomez Iglesias."

"Not by himself!" She tried to sit up.

"Of course not." Jeremy gently pushed her back to the pillows. "He's part of a task force. FBI, US Marshals, ATF and DEA."

She squeezed his hand. "You wish you were with them."

Jeremy gave a one-shoulder shrug. "Yeah, a little. But my responsibility is to protect South Padre Island and you. Thanks to your brilliant skills, they know exactly where Gomez Iglesias and his crew are so I don't think they will have any problems taking them into custody."

She shook her head, not able to track what he was saying, then she winced as pain shot through her temples. "My skills?" She hadn't done anything.

"Your phone. You hid it well."

Right. More memories flooded her brain. Oh no. "He has Amber. And three other young women."

Something flashed in Jeremy's eyes. Then he nodded. "We thought as much but you've confirmed it. I will make sure the information is relayed to the task force."

Her breath hitched. "Gomez is not the cartel boss. His older brother, Ricardo Suarez, is the one in charge."

Surprise flared in Jeremy's eyes. "You saw Ricardo? He's Gomez's brother?"

"Yes. Ricardo was on the yacht." She shivered as the image of Ricardo's slimy smile played across her mind. "Gomez is a horrible man, but his brother... Ricardo's diabolical."

"Not many live who've seen Ricardo." Jeremy stood. "I need to let the task force know."

He moved out of the room. She glimpsed a uniformed guard standing outside. The doctor and a nurse came in, drawing her focus. Dr. Gravites, whose name was stitched onto his white lab coat, did a thorough examination. The nurse redressed her wound. They gave her something for the pain.

"Your vitals are good," Dr. Gravites said after listening to her lungs and heart.

Her gaze went to the door. Where was Jeremy? "When can I leave here?"

"I want to do a CT scan and some blood work," the doctor replied. "If all those come back clean, then I'd say by the morning."

A few minutes after the doctor and nurse left, Jeremy returned.

"When will Tarren be back?"

Jeremy sat and considered her with a knowing look in his eyes. Her stomach clenched.

"He'll be back when he's back," Jeremy stated firmly. "And I know you will be the first person he will want to see."

She held her brother's gaze. "I love him, Jeremy. Are you going to be okay with that? Him being your best friend and employee and all."

"Yes. I can live with it." Her brother chuckled. "I suspected as much. And I think he's got it bad for you, too. I've never seen him so…" Jeremy shook his. "He wouldn't leave your side until the doctors promised you were going to be okay."

Her heart stalled, then beat in big booming, overjoyed thumps.

Jeremy took her hand again. "Jules, Tarren's life wasn't easy growing up."

"He told me about his mother's drinking," she said. Her heart ached for the little boy Tarren had been. But he was a man now and she wanted nothing more than to spend the rest of her life loving him.

"He did?" Jeremy's expression turned thoughtful. "Then you know he has baggage that has kept him from making any commitments."

"He's committed to his job and our family. Just as you are," she countered.

"But we have great parents," he said.

"We do." She longed to see her mom and dad and worried how they would react when they found out what had happened. "Believe me, I know it's a risk to open up to someone when you've been hurt."

Jeremy's gaze darkened. "You're talking about Bryce. I'd like to give him a piece of my mind."

Though she appreciated her brother's fierce loyalty, she said, "We all have hurts in our lives that we can choose to hang on to or let go of. Like you with Kara."

His expression hardened. "We're not talking about me."

Her brother wasn't ready to let go of his hurt over being dumped by Kara, his high school sweetheart. Maybe someday but not today. "I'm hoping Tarren will be willing to take the risk on love rather than let the past ruin his future."

She sent up a prayer that the man she loved would hurry back to her.

Jeremy leaned forward to place a kiss on her forehead. "I love you, sis. And Tarren would be a fool not to realize what he could have with you."

Having her brother's blessing filled her with so much pleasure that all the pain in her body receded to a dull ache. "Thank you."

"I have to warn you." Jeremy pulled a face. "Mom and Dad are on their way."

Happy to hear it, she cocked her head. "How—?"

Jeremy rolled his eyes. "It's been all over the news."

Ah. Maxwell. The island's reporter who did his job with dogged determination.

Her brother smiled at her. "Life in a small island town."

She'd never wanted attention, especially not such public notice. But it was a small price to pay to have found a love worth fighting for. As her eyelids grew heavy, and fatigue coaxed her back to oblivion, she lifted a prayer that God would keep Tarren safe and bring him back to her in one piece.

Seated in the rear passenger seat of a black SUV, Tarren hung up the phone from his call with Jeremy. Hearing that Julia was awake and lucid eased the constriction in Tarren's chest. Learning they'd been correct in their assumption that the Rio Diablo Cartel had kidnapped Amber Lynn along with several other women made his blood boil.

From the far back compartment, Raz let out a huff.

Tarren glanced over his shoulder. "Settle."

The dog just stared back at him. Raz wasn't over being made to sit on the sidelines when Tarren had fought Cinco. Or being left on the boat when Tarren had jumped into the ocean to rescue Julia.

Sitting beside Tarren on the back passenger bench seat was Deputy US Marshal Sera Morales-O'Brien and on her other side sat Deputy US Marshal Lucas Cavendish. In the front passenger seat was Deputy US Marshal Jace Armstrong, and behind the wheel was Deputy US Marshal Brian Forrester. The marshals service operating out of San Antonio had shown up in force when FBI Special Agent in Charge Clark Whitman had put out the call to populate an emergency task force to take down the Rio Diablo Cartel.

Clark and three more FBI agents rode in an SUV in front of the one Tarren now sat in, and behind Tarren and the marshals, were two more SUVs filled with ATF and several members of the Federal Ministerial Police, Mexico's equivalent of the FBI.

In a caravan line, the vehicles climbed a dirt road up a hillside toward the compound where Gomez Iglesias and Ricardo Suarez were holed up, some twenty miles south of Vera Cruz, Mexico.

The FBI had been working closely with the Mexican federal police to bring down the Rio Diablo Cartel. When the FBI reached out with the location of where the yacht had docked, the FMP was more than happy to accept help in taking down one of both countries' most active human traffickers. The team had raided the yacht, but it had been empty. Now they were set to raid the compound.

Sera's eyebrows hitched upward. "Good news?"

"That was my boss," Tarren told them. He refrained from mentioning that Jeremy was also his best friend and the brother of the woman he loved. "The witness can place Ricardo Suarez on the yacht along with Gomez Iglesias. Apparently, they are brothers."

In the front passenger seat, Jace twisted around to stare at him. Surprise evident on his face beneath the brim of his tan cowboy hat. "Brothers. That explains a lot."

"How so?" This from the driver, Brian.

Jace turned to face the front window. "I've heard that Ricardo Suarez doesn't tolerate mistakes. He has done away with more of his own men than he has law enforcement. Seems he tolerates his brother."

"But if the witness—" Sera glanced at Tarren. "Julia, right?"

"Yes, Julia." Just saying her name brought a dose of pleasure to Tarren's heart.

"Until we take Ricardo into custody, she's still in danger," Lucas supplied.

Worry chomped through Tarren. But he trusted Jeremy would keep her safe. He sent up a prayer asking God to keep watch over them all.

"Ricardo Suarez makes Tomas Garcia look like a kitten," Jace said in a grave tone.

Tarren remembered when the US Marshals had taken down the Garcia Cartel a couple of years ago. There had been some close calls. "My boss will keep her safe."

"Who's going to keep your boss safe?" Brian muttered from the driver's seat.

Acid bubbled in Tarren's stomach. "I suggest we make sure that we get Ricardo and Gomez and that we put them somewhere where they can never hurt anyone again."

"I'm sure the FBI has a black site we can drop them in," Jace said. He twisted around to look at Tarren. "Unless you had something of a more permanent placement in mind."

Tarren made a face. "Only if absolutely necessary."

"Agreed," Jace said. "But sometimes you have no choice."

Tarren had a feeling Jace was speaking from experience, but the Rio Diablo compound loomed ahead at the top of the cliff overlooking the Gulf of Mexico and drew everyone's attention.

The tiered, stately home, made of white stucco, basked in sunlight and appeared as if carved into the face of the hillside. Lush foliage hid what Tarren knew was an electrified fence. They'd viewed satellite photos on the plane ride down from Texas and had deemed the best course of action to make a frontal breach through the main gate.

The SUV's radio crackled. Brian picked up. "Forrester here. Go."

Special Agent in Charge Clark Whitman's voice came through the car speaker. "Let's keep this tight. Once we get through the gate, then expect chaos to reign."

"Copy that," Brian said, switching off the radio.

"Okay." Sera rubbed her hands together. "Let's do this."

"Remember," Tarren said. "There are civilians here that need rescuing."

At least he hoped Amber and the other women would be inside the compound and not already moved out of their reach.

Ahead of them, the black SUV carrying the

FBI agents rammed the large metal gate. Sparks flew. The gate held for a moment. Tarren sucked in a breath and sat at the edge of his seat. His hands gripped the AR-15 rifle strapped across his body, the barrel pointing at the roof of the SUV. Would this work?

The lead SUV broke through the gate. The big metal pieces fell to the sides. Brian drove their SUV through the opening, following closely behind the other SUV. A hailstorm of bullets riddled the SUVs as they came to a halt in the wide parking area, behind three luxury SUVs and a sports car.

The rest of the task force's SUVs roared to a stop alongside the first two SUVs, blocking the exit so that no one from the compound could escape by car.

Kind of dumb of Ricardo to have only one way in and one way out. Though if the rumors were true about the man being overly cautious and wily, Tarren was sure Ricardo had an escape route.

But Tarren's focus was Gomez. And finding the women who had been taken. He would let the others deal with a cartel boss.

Hopping out of the SUV and using the door for cover, Tarren returned fire, wounding two guards on one of the terraces and taking them out of commission. He whistled for Raz. The dog scrambled over the backrest of the bench seat and hopped out of the vehicle. Quickly attaching a long leash to the dog's collar, Tarren called out, "We're going in."

Someone replied, "We'll lay down cover fire."

With Raz at his side, Tarren ran into the lower level of the house. Several agents and the marshals followed. Moving in tandem with Raz, Tarren found a door and kicked it in. They rushed into what appeared to be a pantry. Leading with the business end of his automatic rifle, Tarren entered the kitchen.

The kitchen staff huddled together, covering their heads. They were all dressed in uniform black pants and white shirts.

"Someone get them out of here," one of the marshals instructed as they filed in behind Tarren.

Tarren tugged one of the male waitstaff to his feet and pushed him up against the wall. "Where is Gomez Iglesias?"

SEVENTEEN

Frustration pounded through Tarren's brain as the man shook his head. He obviously didn't know where Gomez Iglesias was, or he didn't understand Tarren's question.

Raz growled as if to prompt a response from the man.

Tarren tried a different question. "Where are the women?"

The man continued to shake his head, his gaze darting to Raz.

An older, heavyset woman with years of lines on her face rose to her feet with some effort. "He doesn't speak English," she said in very good English. "The women you seek are on the top floor, the last bedroom. You arrived in time. That monster would have sold them, and they would be forever lost."

Brian tapped Tarren on the back. "We're on it." He and Sera hustled out of the kitchen with two FMPs and an FBI agent following close behind them.

Releasing the man he held, Tarren stepped over to the old woman. "And Gomez Iglesias? Where is he?"

"He did not return with Ricardo." She shrugged. "I have no idea. But that one, you don't want to mess with."

The breath squeezed out of Tarren's lungs. Gomez wasn't here. Was the woman to be believed? Maybe she was protecting him.

Clark, flanked by more FMP and FBI agents, demanded to know, "Where's Ricardo Suarez?"

"He's gone. There are tunnels that he uses to come and go from," she said. "I doubt you'll find him."

Of course there was an escape route. Tarren's fists clenched. "Where do we access the tunnels?"

"I've never seen them, I've only heard about them," the old woman replied. "I'm just the cook."

Holding Raz's leash so the dog stayed close, Tarren and Clark raced from the room as other agents hustled the old woman and the others out of the kitchen and into the yard.

"We have to find those tunnels," Clark said as they hurried into the living quarters of the elaborately decorated dwelling. "We can't let him get away again."

Tarren and Clark met up with FMPs who had taken several of Ricardo's men into custody.

One of the FMP officers said in English, "Ricardo Suarez is not here."

Clark turned to the cartel members now sitting on the ground with their hands cuffed behind their backs. "Where are the tunnels?"

The men remained mute.

One of the FMPs said something in Spanish that Tarren only caught a couple of words— *prison* and *death*.

One of the cartel men said, "The boss has an opening through his walk-in closet. Behind his shoe rack."

Hoping the intel was good, Tarren raced up the wide marble staircase. At the top of the stairs, he met up with Jace, Brian, Sera and Duncan.

"We found the young ladies," Jace said. "Agents took them out already. They were unharmed."

Tarren was thankful for that and couldn't wait to tell Julia, but first, they needed to stop Ricardo and find Gomez.

Clark explained the situation.

They spread out, looking through the rooms trying to find the boss's suite. Tarren opened the door at the end of the hall on the top floor. The bedroom inside was opulent in gold and red, with a four-poster bed and a large television covering one wall. A large, gilt-framed oil painting of Ricardo Suarez hung over the bed.

From behind Tarren, Sera snorted. "The man's not narcissistic at all."

Seeing the humor but not sparing a moment

to respond, Tarren dashed across the room to the large walk-in closet. The man had three shoe racks. Who needed that many shoes? Tarren yanked each rack away from the wall until he found the entrance to the tunnels. A door with a small handle opened to a string of lights hung from the ceiling, illuminating the rough-hewn dirt passageway.

Before leaving the closet, Tarren grabbed a shoe and held it out to Raz. The dog sniffed the high-end leather. "Find." Tarren gave the command and let Raz guide the way into the tunnels that descended at a slope. They came to a fork, and the tunnels diverged. Both directions were lit up with strings of ceiling lights.

Jace stopped next to Tarren. "What is it with these cartel guys and tunnels?"

Sensing a tale there, Tarren slanted him a glance. "You've had some experience?"

"A story for another time," Jace said. "Does your dog have a scent?"

Tarren regarded Raz, who pulled to the right, the leash stretching taut. "This way."

With Raz taking point, his nose twitching in the musty-smelling air, the group veered to the right. Tarren realized the tunnel's slope had become steeper and the earth damper. His ears popped. The briny scent of the ocean permeated the man-made underground passage.

To Clark, Tarren said, "We need someone to find the other end of the cave."

Clark spoke in rapid Spanish to their Mexican colleagues. One of them got on their radio and gave the request.

Raz let out a low growl.

Tarren gave a soft whistle, bringing Raz to his side. Putting his finger to his lips, Tarren made a shushing sound. If they were gaining on their target, he didn't want to alert Ricardo.

Up ahead, light spilled into the tunnel. The opening loomed. The roar of the ocean washing up onto the shore filled Tarren's ears.

They broke out of the cave-like end of the tunnel onto the beach.

Ricardo Suarez ran toward a motorized pontoon boat.

"Take out the boat," Clark yelled, then repeated the directions in Spanish.

Gunfire erupted around Tarren. The boat listed to the side as the rubber siding was struck by bullets.

Ricardo changed directions, running toward the marina where his yacht was moored.

Intent on capturing Ricardo because he could tell Tarren where Gomez was, Tarren and Raz raced after the cartel boss.

The marshals were hot on their heels.

When they were within twenty feet of their

prey, Tarren came to an abrupt halt and undid Raz's tether, then gave the command "Bite."

It was all the impetus Raz needed. The dog streaked through the sand, past the marshals, and launched himself at Ricardo, sending the man to his knees with a scream of outrage. Raz then latched onto Ricardo's arm and dug his paws into the soft sand.

Releasing his sidearm, Tarren ran up and then gave the command for Raz to release his bite. "Out."

The dog immediately obeyed but stood his ground, barking at Ricardo. Tarren reclipped the leash to Raz's collar as law enforcement created a tight circle around their suspect.

"Hands behind your back," Jace yelled at Ricardo.

The man whimpered but complied. One of the FMPs slapped handcuffs around Ricardo's wrists and hauled him to his feet.

"Wait. *Un momento*," Tarren said to the FMP officers. Then he focused on Ricardo. "Where's your brother, Gomez?"

Ricardo's face, smeared with sand and dirt from his face-plant, smiled. The pure evil there sent a chill down Tarren's spine.

"You see, the thing about my brother is," Ricardo said in cultural tones, "he holds a grudge when his plans go awry. And he won't rest until he exacts his revenge."

Ricardo's words sent panic ricocheting through Tarren. He had to get home. He had to get to Julia.

Ten hours later, Tarren and Raz stepped out of the elevator and onto the fourth floor of the hospital in South Padre Island.

Down at the end of the hall, two uniformed police officers stood guard before a closed door.

Julia.

Eager anticipation buzzed along Tarren's nerve endings.

He scanned the floor; nothing seemed out of the ordinary. When he'd called Jeremy from the plane, his boss and best friend had assured him that Julia was well protected. Trying to slow his heart rate and his breathing, Tarren walked in tandem with Raz down the hallway, garnering questioning looks from the doctors, nurses and patients.

From a side hallway, a medical tech, dressed in scrubs with a surgical mask over his face and a cap covering his head, stepped into the main hallway and pushed a cart in the direction of Julia's room.

Raz let out a low growl. The hairs on the back of Tarren's neck shivered. He hurried his steps until he was even the man.

Raz's growl intensified.

The medical tech glowered down at Raz with a frown. "He shouldn't be in here."

The heavily accented voice flooded wary caution through Tarren's system. He stepped into the medical tech's path. "I need to see some ID."

The guy grunted and tried to push past Tarren. But Tarren wouldn't budge. The man lifted his gaze. Tarren sucked in a breath.

The same dark cold eyes as Ricardo Suarez.

"Gomez Iglesias," Tarren said, as he unclipped the safety strap over his weapon but didn't draw his sidearm. He hoped to take Gomez into custody without firing a shot. "Put your hands on your head."

Gomez shoved the cart at Tarren and lumbered down the hall toward the elevator. The two police officers moved to give chase, but Tarren held up a hand, keeping them in place.

Tarren pushed the cart out of the way, released his hold on the leash and gave Raz the command "Bite."

Raz raced down the hallway, his nails clicking on the linoleum floor. People jumped out of the way.

The elevator dinged and the doors opened, and Jeremy stepped out.

"Gomez!" Tarren shouted.

Correctly reading the situation, Jeremy moved into Gomez's path, pushing the man back just as Raz reached Gomez and latched onto his arm.

Gomez let out a guttural scream.

"Out." Tarren gave the release command and Raz let go of his quarry.

Within moments, Tarren and Jeremy had Gomez Iglesias in handcuffs and on his knees. Raz danced with triumph. Tarren didn't blame him. He wanted to dance as well.

To Jeremy, Tarren said, "He's all yours."

Tarren clicked into his cheek, indicating for Raz to follow, and they hurried down the corridor to Julia's door. Tarren was grateful to see the two uniformed police officers hadn't left their post. He saluted them as he entered the room.

The door opened. Expecting the doctor to tell her she was cleared to be discharged, Julia was stunned to see Tarren and Raz step inside and close the door behind them.

"You're here!" She couldn't keep the joy exploding in her chest from her voice.

Tarren's gaze zeroed in on Julia, propped up in the hospital bed. Heat crept up her cheeks as he continued to stare. She touched a hand to her hair, smoothing out the tangles. She, no doubt, looked frightening.

Clearing his throat, Tarren moved forward with Raz at his side. They came to a stop at the foot of the bed. "I'm here."

She glanced past him toward the closed door. "What was all that commotion?"

"Just taking out the garbage," he said with grim satisfaction ringing in his tone. "You will no longer be in danger from the Rio Diablo Cartel."

Good news indeed. "Gomez and Ricardo have been captured?"

"They have."

Wariness crimped her chest. "Amber and the other young women?"

"Safe and sound," he replied. "And on their way to their respective families."

Breathing a giant sigh of relief, she held out her hand.

Slowly, he stepped to the side of the bed and grasped her hand. Raz went up on his hind legs, putting his paws on the edge of the bed as if he, too, wanted to hold her hand.

"Now you can resume your life without worry," Tarren said.

Her fingers curled through his. "I don't want to go back to my old life."

Surprise flared in his gaze. "You don't?"

"No. I was lonely and hurting." Pouring all the love and affection she could into her eyes, she held his gaze. "I was letting the past isolate me from everyone I love. I don't want to do that anymore. I want to live in the present and hope for the future with the man I love."

His expression shuttered. She understood he would need some coaxing.

She squeezed his hand. "In case I wasn't clear, I love you, Tarren."

"What if something goes wrong?" His voice broke.

The pain in his dark eyes formed a lump in her throat.

"There are so many unknowns here," he said and tried to break the contact of their hands, but she held on tight.

"What if I bail like my father did when things got tough?" he continued, his tone bleak. "Or I turn to alcohol like my mother?" He shook his head. "I can't risk hurting you."

Tears gathered in her eyes, blurring her vision, and she tightened her hold on his hand. "We aren't in control of the future. Only God is. But with Him on our side, Tarren, we can get through anything. I'm confident you will choose love over escaping."

For a long moment, he stared at her. She gave him time to wrestle with the demons of his past. Finally, a smile broke out over his handsome face and his body seemed to relax. "I love you, Julia. I think I have loved you most of my life."

"Me, too!" A giggle of delight escaped. "I've loved you most of my life." She tugged at his hand to draw him closer. "You made me a promise. Remember?"

His smile turned into a grin that had her toes curling under the hospital bedsheets.

"I did," he said, his tone low and husky. "And I do."

He leaned down and pressed his lips to hers. Her free hand came up and tangled in his hair, drawing him even closer. She reveled in the sensation of his mouth covering hers, of the taste of his love and the knowledge that she would never be alone again.

Behind them, the door opened. Tarren broke the kiss and straightened. She let out a growl of frustration. Her brother hovered in the doorway. Raz went to Jeremy for a pet.

Jeremy cocked an eyebrow, his gaze bouncing between Tarren and Julia.

Tarren gathered her hand in his and faced Jeremy. "I love your sister. You okay with it?"

Jeremy laughed a deep and joyous sound. When he finally gained control of his humor, he pointed at Julia. "She asked almost the same thing."

Julia grinned at her brother and squeezed Tarren's hand. "He's okay with it."

Jeremy rushed forward and held out his hand. "Welcome, officially, to the family."

Tarren took his hand. "You all have been more of a family to me than I could've ever hoped for."

Jeremy took him in for a quick embrace. Then he stepped back. "I couldn't ask for anyone better for my little sister."

Julia cleared her throat, drawing both men's

attention. She made a shooing gesture with her hand. "You can leave now, Jeremy."

Chuckling and, clearly, not taking offense, Jeremy nodded and left the room.

As soon as the door shut behind him, Julia said, "I'd like another kiss, please."

Raz jumped onto the bed and licked her face.

Laughing, she put her arms around the dog's neck. Careful of where he'd sustained his earlier injury, she met the dog's dark eyes. "That wasn't what I had in mind. But I appreciate your effort."

"Scoot over," Tarren said.

Releasing Raz, Julia adjusted herself on the bed, making space for Tarren. Raz walked to the end of the bed and settled down on her feet.

Stretched out beside her on top of the covers, Tarren took her into his arms. "About that kiss—"

He lowered his mouth to hers and she delighted in the love they shared, and the wonderful future stretched out before them.

* * * * *

*If you liked this story from Terri Reed,
check out her previous
Love Inspired Suspense books,*

Search and Detect
Shielding the Innocent Target
Undercover Christmas Escape
Explosive Trail
Forced to Hide

*Available now from Love Inspired Suspense!
Find more great reads at
www.LoveInspired.com.*

Dear Reader,

One of the great aspects of being a writer is research. While trying to find the perfect setting for this new book and series, I came across a YouTube video of baby sea turtles being released on South Padre Island. From there, I learned everything I could about South Padre Island and sea turtles. I quickly decided I wanted to write a story set on a barrier island in the Gulf of Mexico. And it had to have turtles, which required a character who worked with the turtles. Julia Hamilton was born. She was sensitive, kind and smart, and had such a love for the turtles. Pairing Julia with her older brother's best friend, whom she'd had a crush on since she was a kid, was super entertaining.

Though Safe Haven Turtle Sanctuary in my story is fictitious, I patterned my turtle center after Sea Turtle Inc., which was founded on South Padre Island in 1977 and is dedicated to public education, conservation and rehabilitation of sea turtles. After writing this book and learning about the hatchings, one of my bucket list items is to travel to South Padre Island when the turtles are released. Doesn't that sound like a blast?

To stay informed on upcoming books, join my newsletter at https://www.terrireed.com/

Until next time,
Terri Reed

HARLEQUIN
Reader Service

Enjoyed your book?

Try the perfect subscription for Romance readers and get more great books like this delivered right to your door.

See why over 10+ million readers have tried Harlequin Reader Service.

Start with a Free Welcome Collection with free books and a gift—valued over $20.

Choose any series in print or ebook.
See website for details and order today:

TryReaderService.com/subscriptions